SKYSHIPS OVER INNSMOUTH

Susan Laine

DSP PUBLICATIONS

Published by
DSP PUBLICATIONS

5032 Capital Circle SW, Suite 2, PMB# 279, Tallahassee, FL 32305-7886 USA
www.dsppublications.com

Skyships Over Innsmouth
© 2016 Susan Laine.

Cover Art
© 2016 Stef Masciandaro.
http://www.stefmasc.com/
Cover content is for illustrative purposes only and any person depicted on the cover is a model.

ISBN: 978-1-63476-989-1
Digital ISBN: 978-1-63476-990-7
Library of Congress Control Number: 2016901926
Published August 2016
v 1.0

Printed in the United States of America
∞

This paper meets the requirements of
ANSI/NISO Z39.48-1992 (Permanence of Paper).

This tale of horror is dedicated to the works of H. P. Lovecraft, who introduced a teenaged me to realistic yet dreamlike universes of madness and terror, and to his many fans who joined me on the journey. Thank you.

CHAPTER 1

THE LANTERNS and gaslights flickered in the rough, cold winds, casting lively tricks of light and shadow all around. Dev hugged his wool cloak tighter around his neck. He despised deck duty on bleak evenings like this, when the cold bit like winter—though in reality it was still autumn. But no one was exempt from a shift at the helm, not even Dev, for all he was the captain of this scout airship. He couldn't wait for Stork to relieve him so he could retire to his bunk for the night and dream of… impossible things.

The two-story airship was small enough to enable him to peek at the earth below while manning the wheel. The sun had set moments ago. The horizon still blazed orange, but the land beneath was pitch-black. No lights anywhere.

Dev harrumphed. No people anywhere. Not since the Cataclysm.

The door to the cabin opened at Dev's back, and someone stepped out, audibly protesting the chill. Dev knew whom to expect without looking.

"Good evening, Shay," Dev said, a half smile curling his lips.

The young man grunted. "What's so great about it, Captain Endeavor?" In that moment, Shay sounded nothing like the shining sunbird that had given him his chosen nickname. In fact, his current disposition was the opposite of sunny and shiny.

Dev shrugged, mostly to aggravate the young scholar he liked to tease. "Beautiful sunset, cool winds, smooth sailing. What's not to love?"

Shay inched closer to the railing, back to Dev, trembling under his thick but far too small cloak.

He was slender and short, with shoulder-length wavy blond hair, a few strands of which had escaped the ribbon he had used to tie back his tresses. *Tresses?* Dev briefly considered choosing another word, even in thought. Could one call a man's hair tresses? Well, one word fit as well as the next—for a man with a limited vocabulary.

Dev mentally compared himself to Shay, imagining what the two of them looked like side by side. Where Shay was small, Dev was big, robust, muscular, and hairy, dressed in coarse clothes that barely fit his massive size. He kept his wild black mane cut short, hating when it obstructed his sight and tickled the sides of his face, and his beard neatly trimmed to keep his chin warm without irritating him.

Shay wore simple but elegant clothes. His father must have been wealthy back in the day, for Shay had grown up on a sprawling estate with access to food and clothes sufficient to provide for him in a newly inhospitable world.

Dev had not been as fortunate. He'd grown up in a shelter with dozens of other children like him, lost souls who had not been reunited with their families. But he had never allowed his misfortune to overwhelm him. Whatever strengths and virtues his parents had bestowed upon him, Dev had utilized them all to become the man he was today—an airship captain in his own right.

Shay peered at the countryside below, his brow furrowed. "Anything?"

"Nothing." Dev shook his head even though Shay faced away from him. "What did you expect? Candlelight vigils? Burning cities?"

Shay seemed unwilling to rise to the bait. As he leaned cautiously over the railing, his expression remained glum, almost yearning. "Both. Neither. I don't know. Something. Anything. Proof we were here once."

Dev heard what Shay left unsaid. Here before the Cataclysm. "It's been twenty-three winters. If there was anyone else still alive, the scouts would have found them by now."

"I don't know," Shay said slowly. "It's a big world out there. Earth, I mean."

That, at least, was true. Dev scanned the darkening horizon with no small amount of anxiety. From maps made before the Cataclysm, it was clear the world had grown small in those days, every nook and cranny discovered and occupied. But now it was all unknown again.

Wracking his brain, Dev sought the elusive memories of *before*. But nothing other than a vast black emptiness lay where his memories should have been.

Sighing, Dev wished he recalled even a glimpse of his life before he awoke as a nine-year-old boy in a room full of other children, all as distressed and at a loss as he. Later he learned the building was called a school. But his lost memory provided no connections to the word.

No one's had. Their past? Erased from existence.

Shaking himself out of his gloomy reverie, Dev said, "You weren't even born when the Cataclysm happened. Why did you sign up for this expedition?"

Shay regarded him over his shoulder, silent and solemn, but also curious. "Why not? The world is as unknown to me as it is to anyone else. I may have been born to a world that had lost it all, but I have the same questions buried within me as you do."

Dev turned the steering wheel an inch to the left, more on instinct than at the advice of his sextant or compass. The big helium-filled balloon above him billowed, the thick fabric rippling slightly as the breeze brushed against it.

When Shay turned to observe him, Dev sensed his eyes on him. "Do you know how to read?" Shay asked.

Dev nodded without looking at Shay. "Yes. I was still able to learn. I was young when the Cataclysm happened. Older folks weren't so lucky." He still remembered how hard reading and writing had been after he'd found himself sitting at his school desk, awake but with no memory of what had come before. The odd squiggles in books and on the schoolhouse walls meant nothing to him. But over time he'd managed. "Speaking came easier, though."

Shay smiled ruefully. "I understand. Humanity might have forgotten everything from before, but pride remains. Older folks have found it hardest to adjust, I think, having to endure the embarrassment of being taught how to talk, read, and write by the younger generations."

This was nothing new as far as Dev was concerned. "Time and tide wait for no man." He'd read the quote on a piece of paper in a library when he'd seen seven winters after the Cataclysm. It seemed appropriate to describe how the world did not stop even though humans found themselves at a standstill. Pure as the driven snow they'd been.

"We all had to learn new skills," he commented dryly.

Shay snickered. "Every skill was new back then. Thankfully, we have advanced since then, I think."

Another truth. Nothing had worked back then, so humanity had to rebuild from scratch, to start anew. It had been hard. Heck, it still was. Maybe in a century….

Dev decided it was high time to change the sad subject. Talking about the Cataclysm depressed him. Unless they could all travel back in time—which they couldn't—it was worthless contemplation of what would never come to pass.

"So where are we heading again?" Dev knew the answer, but he longed to speak about the future, not a past that no longer mattered.

Shay swiveled, scanning their surroundings with his sharp eyes. "A small coastal town by the name of Innsmouth."

"Right." Dev shivered for some reason, chills going up and down his spine.

"Yes. Innsmouth, Massachusetts." Shay pronounced the last word very slowly. It was a complex word, with lots of hissing sounds. Most uncomfortable. Dev wouldn't have even tried such a ridiculous-sounding word, known only thanks to maps in schools, libraries, what used to be government buildings, archives, and post offices.

Shay's eyes glowed as he successfully managed to enunciate the difficult word. Dev liked that look on him and smiled.

Swallowing hard, Dev squelched the silly feeling inside him. Even when he had woken after the Cataclysm, he'd felt different. He liked other boys. Well, mostly. Sometimes he liked girls too. But more rarely.

The newspapers discovered after the Cataclysm spoke of a harsh world where those who liked their own sex were regarded poorly and violently, with bigotry and prejudice. But no one could remember why that hatred had existed, so like many other things, it was put aside in favor of rebuilding a global society. Sort of. Shelters and hovels were the most people could manage to build these days. The majority of people lived in the big cities, where defenses had been constructed to protect people from the growing wilderness.

It had been hard when nothing worked. In huge cities, they were surrounded by odd devices that didn't function. Machines, they were called. Some of these machines had buttons, levers, and toggles, but pushing, switching, or flipping them did nothing. So they too were abandoned in favor of relearning the basics—how to talk and interact, how to find food, water, and shelter, and if there was a way to determine who was related to whom.

It had been a chaotic time.

Sometimes Dev couldn't believe over twenty winters had passed since then.

"You're brave," Dev said, hoping Shay would look at him again. "I know it's not easy to be out here."

Shay snorted without glancing at him, and Dev swallowed his disappointment.

"As if it is any easier in other places. Canal City, for instance. Billions died in the upheavals after the Cataclysm. The surviving populace of a few million had nothing, and life is still a struggle. Yes, there's shelter and safety in numbers, but there's a shortage of food, water, clothes, medicines, pretty much every bare necessity. Out here… it's serene and wild. You know, quiet."

Dev was about to point out it was the calm of the grave but bit down the words. He'd come to view all the traveling the scout ships engaged in as a hopeful endeavor, which was why Endeavor was the name he'd chosen for himself to replace the forgotten name he'd been given at birth. He still believed in a brighter future.

Despite the fact nine out of ten places they had visited in the past ten years had turned up empty and abandoned, ransacked, or destroyed—decimated graveyards.

He still had faith, even if he'd most likely spend his days alone, without a warm body next to him in the dead of night, without someone to call his own, to love and be loved by.

He sighed inwardly and stared at Shay's unmoving back, both of them silent.

"Did you see if Stork was up?" Dev asked finally, needing to hear Shay's vibrant voice in all the lifelessness surrounding them.

Shay snickered. "Sleeping in the galley with a bottle of moonshine. Again."

"Where the heck does he keep finding new places to hide those infernal things?" Dev shook his head, grumbling under his breath in dissatisfaction.

Admittedly Stork was much older than any of them. He'd probably seen more than fifty winters in his forgotten lifetime. But he had signed up for this mission of exploration, so he had to contribute along with everyone else. There were only the five of them—Dev, Shay, Malia, Stork, and Wren. They all needed to pull their weight.

Shay looked back at Dev, grinning. "Shall I go and wake him up? I'll be ever so gentle."

Dev chuckled. "I'll give him a boot up his ass if he doesn't show up soon."

Shay's smile slowly faded, and his blue eyes got a faraway look, glazing over. "We've been out here for a long time, haven't we?"

Dev had to admit that was true. This was his and Shay's seventh trip together in the past two winters. Less of a success story than one might assume. "Yeah."

After that he ran out of things to say. Probably because he wanted to say so much but didn't dare. He liked Shay, and they were friends. Shay was one of the few friends Dev had. Talking about feelings and such would only break their amicable relationship.

Still, he tried once more to change the subject to shake his melancholy mood. "What do you think we'll find in Innsmouth?"

He didn't ask if Shay believed they would find people alive there. Most towns and villages were a mess, with the panicked remnant of their residents in hiding. Worse were the places where the darkness within men reigned supreme and death hung heavy over the blood-soaked land. Barbarism had risen again. Murders, thefts, and rapes were commonplace for people who had no knowledge of anything better, only instinct, want, and need to guide them. During the first upheavals, that was all they'd known. Thankfully things had improved since then, if only by a smidgeon.

"I hope at the very least we'll find libraries intact. We need books now more than ever. Perhaps then we can figure out how to work machines—and what went wrong." Shay's optimism lifted Dev's spirits.

"Have you read many books?" Dev asked, curious. Shay must have because he was an acknowledged scholar, which was a fancy word for someone who could read *and* understand what he read. Being able to recognize the alphabet and words didn't equal understanding.

Shay smiled, happiness evident on his face. "Yes. I've read 314 books."

Dev whistled low. "That's three hundred books more than I've read." A somber mood came down upon him. "At least that I remember."

Shay slipped away from the railing to stand at Dev's side. His smile was encouraging. "Most people have only read a handful of books. It's nothing to feel ashamed of. Libraries are few and far between, and paper books even rarer."

Dev frowned. "I've heard talk among the scholars that people before used weird contraptions to store and gain knowledge. Oh, I can't remember what they're called."

"Com-pu-ters."

Shay enunciated the word perfectly, or so Dev liked to believe, appreciating the soft, sweet cadence of his voice. Briefly Dev imagined how wonderful it would be to wake up to that voice crooning in his ear. Then perhaps Shay's warm, adept hand would inch lower, past his abs and navel to his—Dev visibly shook the ridiculous notions out of his head. This hopeless crush would do neither of them any good.

"Yes, those things." Dev nodded firmly, wanting Shay to see him as smart too, even if he hadn't read hundreds of books.

"That is what we assume," Shay said, sounding skeptical. "Since the parts inside all of the ones we have studied are completely burned, singed, or exploded, there's no way to know. But the manuals speak of vast amounts of knowledge stored in them." He sighed, frustrated if his tone was anything to go by. "But we can't get any of them to work."

Over time, scholars—the younger generations—had learned that the devices required something called electricity. But since all those devices had burned, it seemed electricity was a dangerous route to take. Trying to recreate and harness electricity didn't seem the best course of action, so people had turned to steam power. That, at least, they could control. Some machines could be converted to work on steam, and airships had proved their best, most useful invention, given the importance of transportation. But many gadgets had to be completely reinvented, and the appliances of old abandoned or reutilized as scrap metal.

Shay swayed a little, attesting yet again to his lack of sleep. The young scholar was an excitable sort who preferred to work instead of rest.

"When was the last time you've slept through the night, Shay?" Dev asked, annoyed that their sole source of knowledge on this voyage was practically dead on his feet. "You need a good night's sleep."

Shay pursed his lips in fake irritation, his eyes dancing in mirth. "It's too cold in the cabin."

Dev rolled his eyes. "Then put more wood in the brazier." He liked that word. Brazier. He'd learned it from a book, and found it pleasing. Sometimes words evoked a certain feeling inside him. That word whispered of warmth and flames and safety. He couldn't recall why.

"It'll be a long, chilly night still until we reach Innsmouth," Shay complained good-naturedly. "Unless we find survivors, we might not land before then. I don't want to burn all of our firewood reserves into cinders."

Dev scoffed, a lopsided grin on his lips. "We can make emergency stops to replenish our supplies. No one is going to watch over our shoulders how we spend time out here as long as we get the job done."

Shay smiled, his dimples showing. "You're always so practical, Dev. I don't know what I'd do without you." Then he rose up on his tippy-toes, kissed Dev lightly on the cheek, sauntered toward the cabin door, and vanished inside.

His heart beating almost out of his chest, Dev touched the spot Shay's lips had brushed against. Dev's face was roughened by the harsh weather they encountered flying high, but his skin… yes, his skin remembered.

A kiss. *Shay kissed me.*

Suddenly Dev felt feverish, a fire burning inside his body, in his groin.

When Dev and Shay had met three winters ago, they had become friends immediately. But soon, for Dev at least, it had become more. Every morning, his first thought had been of Shay. Dev couldn't wait to see Shay's eyes dance with mirth at Dev, his sweet smile rising on his lips, his contagious enthusiasm, his bright eagerness, and his endless kindness. Days when they were apart were gray, sad, and pointless. Dev's whole life these days revolved around Shay.

That single spark had grown into a wildfire. Those feelings would engulf Dev in the end, burning his heart and body to ashes. Shay's kiss, an act of friendship alone, didn't help matters.

Now Dev feared he might never be able to live without that touch for the rest of his life—with Shay so close and yet so far, quite beyond his reach.

Shay can never be mine. Not with… Malia onboard. She's a dream come true for any red-blooded man. And despite his youth, Shay is a man. A man who loves a woman.

Dev closed his eyes, a deep, sorrowful pang in his chest, hollowing him out.

"…what are all these kissings worth if thou kiss not me?" Dev mused in silence. Whoever this Shelley person was, he sure hit the nail on the head.

CHAPTER 2

SHAY ENTERED his cramped cabin, blowing out a breath as he leaned against the door. He brushed a hand over his forehead, sweaty and feverish again, just like his nether regions. Not to mention his fast-beating heart that seemed ready to jump out of his throat.

Dev. Dev again. Always Dev.

What on earth had possessed him to kiss Dev? Cursing under his breath, Shay tried to push the rough-stock captain out of his mind. It did no good to dwell on what could never be. But he admitted to himself it was hard to let go. After two winters, with a third closing in, Shay had grown used to Dev and his solitary ways in the Scout and Ranger Corps.

"Did you bring me any wine?" a woman's soft voice called from the back of the cabin where the bed was tucked in an alcove, hidden by a dark red curtain.

Shay suppressed a grimace. "No, Malia. I didn't get the chance to raid the pantry."

A disappointed sound came from behind the curtain. "It's all right. I didn't really want any. I guess I'm a bit bored out here with nothing to do."

Shay frowned. "Not every place can be a battlefield for your entertainment, Malia. You may be itching for a fight to get your blood flowing, but the rest of us seek peace and a chance to reb—"

"A chance to rebuild, yes, I know." She lifted the veil and stood, facing Shay at last.

A tall athletic woman, Malia was beautiful. Her long brown curls cascaded down to her waist in a thick wave; her hazel eyes were pure flames; and her black-clad figure, complete with an ample bosom and round hips tucked under an armored, hourglass-shaped corset, was ever at the ready to start a war—or to end one. Malia was their security for this mission, the stunshine gun she carried around her waist one testament to her station. Not that she needed rifles to defeat her enemies. No, she was gifted in the arts of martial combat too. Malia's talent reigned supreme, making her extremely useful in wilderness or other hazardous explorations.

It was called muscle memory, Shay recalled. The notion of their bodies being able to remember routines or repetitive tasks encouraged Shay because it suggested that though the human race had lost their memories, they had not lost everything. If they had, then there would be no muscle memory or even basic language learning skills. Yet they possessed the ability to relearn communication skills and their bodies recalled past actions. That boded well for their rebuilding efforts.

Malia smiled at Shay, her bloodred lips full and pouty. "Do you think after all this time I don't know your dreams, my darling? I too want to see peace and prosperity restored to our poor downtrodden world. But I am not naïve enough to believe we can do that without shows of force."

Shay looked away, worrying his bottom lip. It was useless to argue with Malia. She'd continue until she alone stood as the victor. Shay might have been a scholar, but when it came to intellectual discourse, Malia still held the upper hand simply because she never recognized loss as an acceptable outcome.

Still, it unnerved him how well she knew him—and his dreams. That was how it had all begun. With dreams. About Dev.

Shay recalled the first time with ease, for he had awoken in the dead of night, sweaty and trembling and afraid for reasons he could not explain. Dev had been a mere shadow in the darkness, but he'd radiated a kind of glow, unmistakable and undeniable. Like dark storm clouds, those gray eyes of his blew Shay away. His smile set Shay's knees shaking, his heart thundering, and his blood roaring. That night Shay had, for the first time, known true want.

Why had it never felt like that with… her?

"Have you been to the deck?" Malia asked, her soft voice granting Shay a pass. Grateful, he nodded. "When will we arrive at our destination?"

"Tomorrow morning, if all goes according to plan," Shay replied.

They'd already been on their way for two days. The airship was capable of good speed, nearly fifty miles per hour. But they traveled at a much lower rate, five miles per hour, so that they could spot any possible survivors on the ground. Depending on the winds and barring any interruptions, their journey to Innsmouth would take approximately three days, then one to three days to explore, and another two to three to get back to Canal City.

Lately Malia had begun to feel like a stone around Shay's neck, pulling him down. Why she had chosen him as the object of her affections he didn't have a clue. At first Shay had been flattered by her attention and fallen hard for her charms. But she had her dubious, occasionally condescending, attitudes—and ethics that bent according to the situation she was in.

In short, Malia was nothing like Dev, whose stout moral backbone and reliable fortitude never wavered. What you saw was what you got. Shay admired Dev's courage of conviction and strong sense of self. Shay wished he could be the same and finally admit to Malia that he no longer cared for her the way he had. But it was hard considering how humanity's numbers had dwindled over the past twenty winters.

Malia sighed and wandered to the porthole. She leaned against it to stare out at the dark night high above the ground. "I suppose we must all gather our patience, then. That and our weapons." She glanced at him over her shoulder. "Do you expect we'll be met with deadly force once we get there?"

"I don't know."

Shay would have wished to be able to say a definite no. But as the chaotic times after the Cataclysm had proved, man could indeed act as predator toward his fellow man. The sudden and inexplicable event that was the Cataclysm caused some people to react violently, in panic and paranoia, and many had died over the first few moons. That number had since escalated into tens of millions, maybe more. If they didn't get their act together soon, the human race could become extinct.

Those who had survived the Cataclysm and the subsequent upheavals had gathered in cities, like their own Canal City, and sought safety in numbers. As the summers and winters had passed, more people had arrived from small towns and villages and faraway settlements, but every winter fewer still, until no one came anymore. Not one in the past three winters.

The Scout and Ranger Corps was created to find and give aid to anyone still out there. City by city and town by town, places on the map were scoured for survivors by legions of airships with ample landing crews. At first a scattered few were discovered and brought to Canal City and other places. Lately, though, only emptiness and destruction had been the reward for their diligence.

"Why are we even going to this godsforsaken place?" Malia asked, her gaze remaining fixed through the porthole.

Her frustration was understandable. Many believed it was time to forget the outside world and shift focus to rebuilding the few remaining cities to their former glory. These search journeys wasted already scarce resources. Aside from rescue of survivors, there were only two other reasons to venture out into the wild: to find and replenish their dwindling resources—food, water, and clothing—and to learn how the Cataclysm had happened, what had caused it, and if it could be reversed.

"Any town still left standing could provide us with resources Canal City desperately needs," Shay replied, his voice tinged with his distaste for her question, one she asked every damn day. "Besides, Innsmouth is special."

"Oh?" Malia asked, though Shay wondered if she really cared.

"The town doesn't show on any official maps," Shay explained, sitting down at the round table where his papers, notes, and maps were laid out. "It's curious how and why so many books mention it, but no maps show it. We've only discovered a couple of rude renderings, hand drawn. Surely a great treasure trove of knowledge must be buried there."

"A secret town," Malia commented, her interest flaring. She left the porthole to come and stand behind Shay. "That sounds promising."

"Yes. If no known maps show Innsmouth, the town could be mostly or entirely intact. A wealth of resources could be found there."

Excitement lifted its pretty head within Shay, as it did every time he contemplated a better future. "Perhaps even survivors."

"Surely not after all this time?" Malia said, her head cocked as she studied the maps from her vantage point.

"Skepticism won't help us here," Shay cut in, a bit more sharply than he intended.

Malia snorted. "A healthy dose of skepticism has kept us alive as long as we have been, my dear. With the wilderness now crawling with marauders and bandits, not to mention wild animals, I'd say a certain reticence is advisable."

She wasn't wrong. But where Shay saw humanity as an entity capable of greatness and improvement, Malia saw the pitfalls of human weaknesses expanded by ignorance and fear. History books in the libraries seemed to show humanity's lack of capability to rise above such things or rise to the occasion, which unfortunately validated Malia's point of view.

"We'll see." Shay jutted his chin in defiance, gritting his teeth, firm in his faith that tomorrow would yield keys to humanity's future, not its demise.

RESTORING THE machines that had been lost proved to be a futile effort. So the machines of conveyance—the ones called cars, busses, trains, and planes—sat in place, with no one able to move or steer them. Constructing new means of transportation proved easier than trying to get the old ones working. They all seemed to have been powered by electricity, which no one knew exactly how to use anymore. Harnessing lightning was seen as a fool's errand.

Dev's steam-powered airship was small and silent, but she glided through the air like a majestic bird. That's why Dev called her the *Smoke Sparrow*. She was an elegant piece of wood with metal reinforcements and a big, dark blue helium balloon above. Two propellers, running on steam and operated by Stork and Wren, moved the airship to wherever her captain wished. Lately that had been solely scouting expeditions.

Though the quarters inside were cramped, forcing Shay to bow his head most of the time, Shay had fallen in love with the nimble little craft the moment he had seen it. Falling for her handsome captain hadn't been far behind.

As he stood next to Dev the next morning, Shay felt the man's arm brush against his every now and then when he turned the steering wheel. The brief contact made Shay's heart flutter. His heated body sought Dev's nearness at every opportunity.

That deep desire confused Shay. After the past two winters, he no longer knew whether his desire to travel with Dev was more about finding new towns or simply being with Dev. Dev's presence made the long nights, moons, and winters passable. Shay wished he could confess his feelings to Dev. But as long as Malia was around, Shay could not. He wasn't a heel, certainly not to the extent of ditching a woman who had meant the world to him once for the promise of a new love.

Besides, perhaps Dev didn't feel the same and would thus never reciprocate Shay's love. The fear of that fate compounded the issue of keeping his feelings a secret. Fear was a powerful master; it rarely, if ever, released its slaves unscathed.

"There!" Dev's voice interrupted Shay's ruminations. Dev was pointing past the bow of the ship to the town up ahead.

Shay stirred with excitement all but bubbling over. No matter how mixed up his feelings were about Dev and Malia, his enthusiasm for new discoveries never dimmed. "Is it Innsmouth?" he asked, shaking with the thrill of revelation.

"It must be. No other towns around here. Closest is Ipswich, and that's a long ways away." Dev grinned at him. "We found it. Let's hope there's more than empty houses and streets, eh?" He nudged at Shay with his shoulder, playful, and Shay laughed. He'd almost forgotten laughter.

Dev stared down at him, a dreamy look in his gray eyes. Then he blinked hard, gave a forced smile, and turned away. Shay swallowed his disappointment. Perhaps he'd only imagined it, seeing the fire blazing in Dev's eyes.

"What do we know about this town?" Dev asked after clearing his throat.

Some of Shay's mirth had subsided, but he felt obliged to offer as much information as he had available. "We don't have much. We believe the town was founded five hundred years ago, in 1643. Over time the town was known for its shipbuilding and fishing industries. They had some odd sort of religion, which we know very little about." He sighed. "I wish more libraries had been spared."

Dev nodded at his side. "Me too."

During the first winter after the Cataclysm, it became obvious that finding warmth was hard. Books were easy to burn, and along with other perishables, they had been the first to go. It was only after surviving the first few winters that people started saving books to learn about the past in the hopes of undoing whatever had gone so horribly wrong.

Nonetheless, many libraries had lost a large portion of their inventories. The Canal City Library was still intact and functioned as their primary storage facility for books and a repository of knowledge gained. Monument City, farther southwest, had another big one, and they had agreed to share whatever they learned during their expeditions.

"What else?" Dev asked as they glided quietly across the skies, with only minor puffs of steam from the engines to mark their passage toward the town. Silent as a tomb it was. The morning sun had shone brightly as the airship made its approach, gliding toward the town like a giant bird, but now the sky was overcast, with a heaviness in the air that Shay felt as pressure in his lungs.

"There was a plague, but that was hundreds of years ago. I'm confident there isn't a trace of it left." Shay put as much conviction into his voice as he could. Sicknesses were a huge threat since medicines were scarce and their effects often unknown. Medical books were few and far between, and the special words in them often undecipherable. That was why the best precaution they could take was to avoid close contact with anyone who appeared diseased or with anything that seemed contaminated.

"Think it's safe to land?" With narrowed eyes, Dev peered at the looming town as if he was searching for signs of danger. Shay understood. If their vessel was damaged beyond their ability to repair, they would be in serious trouble. On foot, out in the newly formed wilderness, they'd never survive a trek back to Canal City.

Shay swallowed hard. It was his call, as this was his area of expertise. "Go around the town a few laps so we can see for ourselves. Any sign of trouble and we leave."

"Understood." Dev steered the airship to glide gently over the town.

The moment Shay saw the dilapidated state of the structures in town, his high hopes came crumbling down. Most of the buildings, all huddled together along a couple of crisscrossing streets and the banks of a river running through it, suffered from the ravages of time—rotting away and, in some cases, even collapsed into bare skeletons of their former glory.

No smoke rose from any chimneys; no fires appeared behind the broken windows; no sounds emerged from the doorways. No birds sang, no people chattered, and no wild animal seeking to forage the area hastened into the woods at the sight of the airship.

Shay shivered and inched closer to Dev without realizing it. Only when Dev wrapped an arm around his shoulders did Shay notice how his search for strength had led him to Dev's welcome embrace.

"It doesn't look very inviting," Shay whispered, for some unknown reason fearing to speak any louder.

Dev seemed equally disturbed by the chilly ambience of the place as he answered in a low voice, "No, it sure doesn't. Do you think we should risk it nonetheless?"

Shay's first instinct, the primal urge deep within him, screamed at him to get away as quickly as humanly possible. The compulsion was so potent, he actually shifted back a step. "I… I… I don't know…. What do *you* think we should do?" He prayed Dev would choose their safety over exploring this bleak, haunted landscape.

Dev seemed conflicted. "The place feels…." He let his voice linger, then vanish as he gulped hard. Apprehension paled his skin, and Shay was certain his own mirrored Dev's. "There's an oppressive feel to this town, like… like something terrible happened here."

Shay agreed with every fiber of his being. Staring at those caved-in roofs, broken brick walls, and gaping holes here and there, Shay trembled. He felt like they were being watched, as if malicious eyes followed their passage from the ground. His untamed imagination must have been playing tricks on him. He wished they'd rise toward the heavens until the sun reappeared from behind the gray cloud face that stood between them and the light.

A sharp laugh echoed in the dead silence, making both men jump.

Malia stood on the deck, in front of the cabin door, her hands on her hips and a wide grin on her face. Apparently the horrendous mood that hung over this deserted area made no impact on her fierceness or resolve.

"Look at you two," she said with a mocking laugh. "Are you mice or men? No room for cowards here." Her gaze swept over the land as though nothing were amiss. "Captain, find us a stable spot to moor the ship, and let's start exploring."

Shay had to intervene. "Malia, look at the state of decay down there. It's unlikely we'll find any survivors, let alone eatable food or drinkable water. And if there is clothing, it'll be in tatters, riddled with moth holes and dust."

Malia looked at him like he'd grown a second head, as though nothing he'd said was intelligible. "Don't be ridiculous. There could very well be items we could use to barter with other cities. How will we know if we don't even bother to look?"

Her scoffing words ate at Shay's fears, thankfully. Just to show Malia he was as brave as she was, Shay declared, "Fine. We'll go down there and see what we can learn. If we have found nothing of any value by sunset, we leave. Is that understood?" He lifted his chin, staring her down, as resolute as he could be.

Malia laughed, tossing her head so her long brown hair whipped around her like a soft cloud. "That's the spirit." She swiveled around on her heels. "I'll go fetch my weapons while you find us a worthy landing site, Captain."

Once Malia vanished into the bowels of the airship, Dev looked at Shay with a quirked eyebrow, definitely amused.

Shay glared at him. "Save it. Just get this ship moored so we can get this over with. I don't want to stay any longer than we have to."

"Aye…, Captain." Dev's chuckle sparked flames inside Shay, who was sure he'd never heard a sexier sound in his life.

But the moment his gaze veered to the seemingly abandoned rustic town, a chill sank right down to his bones and whisked away all heat from his heart and body.

This town that time forgot is a graveyard. I pray it won't be ours.

Chapter 3

"You're mad!"

Malia laughed at Shay's shout from on high. She wasn't afraid of shadows, even if they moved in the corner of her eye. She'd face them dead-on, rifle and sword in hand.

"Don't be so skittish," Malia yelled back. "None of us will live forever."

The rope she held on to creaked as she glided down. Yet it didn't break. She could have used the rope ladder, but she preferred to slide down into hostile territory as fast as possible, one hand free for the use of weapons at all times.

She landed firmly on the grassy ground by the abandoned lighthouse, her leather boots thumping the earth. But there was no echo. Her surroundings appeared to absorb any sound immediately.

Though they had all been less than quiet on approach, nothing and no one stirred upon their arrival. Malia waited a heartbeat, holding her breath, always ready and expecting the worst. At least she wouldn't be surprised or disappointed were the worst to happen.

The harbor formed what was virtually a full circle though from above it had taken the shape of a crescent moon. A few broken-down shacks and cabins lined the narrow cape that ended at a round, rocky point on top of which stood a ramshackle lighthouse. The stonework, once white, was now gray, craggy, and cracked, with seaweed and moss covering the surface in places. A stone barrier formed a breakwater against the rising tides and restless seas.

Malia attached the rope in a cleat hitch to the lighthouse wall, where an iron lantern twisted and bent but held the knot firmly in place. She yanked the rope three times to indicate the others could come down if they so chose, by rope or rope ladder. Being a pioneer in two separate fields—exploration and martial arts—Malia was ever the first person on reconnaissance. The whole town appeared deserted and falling to pieces, so she deemed it safe enough for Dev, at least, to join her.

A minute later, Dev indeed dropped down the rope to stand at her side, he too preferring to keep one hand free during the descent. Like Malia, he carried a stunshine rifle, along with a curved antique sword and at least two hidden knives she knew of.

"Anything?" Dev's voice was tense and cautious, and he spoke in a low, steady tone. He glanced in every direction with every appearance of caution.

"Nothing." Malia scanned their surroundings. The bay stood between their landing spot and the actual town. "Not a blade of grass stirring."

Dev shuddered. "This place gives me the creeps."

Malia felt no such apprehension. She had nerves of steel. There wasn't a ghost town or haunted mansion invented that could make her blood run cold. She said nothing, deeming it useless. Dev would either gain control over his anxiety, or he would not.

"Shay staying on board?" she asked, never letting her gaze veer from the town across the round bay. Though she rarely felt fear, she had an uncanny sense when it came to being watched. No one yet had been able to take her by surprise. Somewhere, in the shade of a broken town, eyes were fixed upon her. Of that she was certain.

"For now," Dev replied, frowning. "The waters are so still. Like cement. Odd."

Malia shrugged. "Essex Bay is supposed to have calm waters. It's an estuary, after all."

"Is that where we are?" Dev asked, a worried tinge to his voice. "The maps Shay's got with him are less than clear about this whole area. Apparently it's mostly marshland, creeks, and low forest-covered hills."

Malia waved her hand dismissively. "You know how it is, Captain. Once people leave a place, it reverts back to wilderness. Besides, all the maps we have are from before the Cataclysm. No way to know how accurate they are after twenty winters with no one around."

"I guess." Dev sounded only marginally assured by the confidence of her tone. "So where do we start?"

Malia nodded toward the street following the curve of the coastline. "I reckon that's Water Street, as mentioned in the maps. If we walk the length of it, we'll keep the bay to one side and the town to the other. If we can't outrun a threat, we may need to swim to get away."

"This is a fishing town," Dev noted with a modicum of amusement. "The locals, if there are any left, could be masterful swimmers."

Malia grinned. "That's what our weapons are for. Let's get moving while we still have daylight."

"Yes." Dev shivered. "I don't want to get caught in this place after dark."

Malia chuckled at his timorous tone but didn't comment.

Keeping her rifle in hand, Malia rounded the lighthouse to find the actual street. It was a dirt path along the sandy reef, but beyond it, where proper mainland began, the street seemed to transform into cobblestone or asphalt. They were too far away to tell properly.

Thankfully Malia didn't have an itchy trigger finger. Nonetheless, she never let down her guard. While she wasn't afraid, proper caution saved lives.

As they braved on ahead, Malia observed the pebbly shoals awash with capsized boats, their rotting boards bristling with barnacles. More half-sunken ships jutted from the bay or lay half-dragged to the shoreline. Shattered lobster pots and twisted wire fish traps dotted the coastline.

Dev had been right. The still waters didn't churn, wave, or even ripple. With an ocean not far from them, that stillness was unsettling, unnatural, and… plain wrong.

On the other side of Water Street rose tiny dilapidated tenements that once must have housed the poor of this town, or perhaps they had functioned as sheds for fishing implements. The shaded doorways oozed an icy atmosphere, revealing nothing beyond the blackness. Malia felt an uneasy vibration traveling along her spine, and the sensation of being watched intensified.

Yet no one came in sight. Not a glimpse of anyone around. No human sounds at all.

Shards of broken glass lay on the ground where windows had shattered over time—by nature or by the hand of man. Malia saw no blood anywhere, so she cautiously ruled the weather the likely suspect. Of course, she knew the lack of vital fluids didn't necessarily rule out human intervention, since only fresh bodily fluids would be visible. Time would tell.

As she peered to her left, out into the bay, she realized one of the nagging sensations came from the fact that the rickety, partially sunk, or entirely broken piers were creaking and whining—though there were no waves to disturb them.

An undercurrent, perhaps? Malia frowned. Was it possible that whatever instinct had whispered into Dev's ear about the unnatural quality of this haunted place was now affecting her? She longed to dismiss the notion. She was no scaredy-cat. Yet she could not dispel the sensation creeping down her spine.

As they cleared the minor tenements and walked along the perimeter of the town proper, Malia took in the size of the place. The coastal town ascended along the slope of a hillside rising above them like the shadow of a giant. Every street climbed from the shore into a cold dimness. Many of the street signs tilted precariously, had fallen to the ground, or were missing altogether.

That's when Malia figured out why the scene suddenly appeared so ominous and spooky. A frosty fog rolled down from the top of the hill far to the west, beyond what they could see, camouflaging more ground as it approached them like a gray wall. There was a chill in the air that could be accounted for by the season being autumn. But when Malia's hair stood on end, she was no longer certain of mere natural forces at play here.

Which was strange since she didn't know of any other forces besides nature.

Dev eyed the town suspiciously too. "That fog looks mighty thick. If we get separated, we might not be able to find each other again by sight alone." He glanced at her, worry evident in his eyes.

"You're the leader of this expedition now that we're on the ground. You think it's safe to venture up there?" He scanned the town towering over them, and he trembled visibly.

"No place is safe anymore," Malia said quietly. It seemed they both sensed the same thing—something was off. To regain control of the situation, instead of letting the situation control her, Malia shrugged. "I doubt it'll get any safer later. The fog be damned." She glanced at him over her shoulder. "Best not to separate, though. Just in case."

Dev nodded with grim resolve and tightened his grip on his rifle.

"THE SIGNPOST says that's Eliot Street," Dev commented quietly, his tense stance indicating that he was as wary as Malia. They had passed several streets winding up the hillside but hadn't yet chosen any of them. Smells of decay and rot pierced the otherwise cool, salty sea air. "According to the maps, that should lead to Main Street. That's usually the most important thoroughfare in any town. Sounds like a place to start. What do you think?"

"Municipal buildings and archives could be there," Malia noted. "And if there are any survivors, they might seek shelter at community buildings. Good call."

Eliot Street, it seemed, was a small diagonal street running upward between two big buildings, both of them mostly fallen apart, with nothing but a few load-bearing walls and stray beams still standing, though happily rotting away and covered in moss and lichen.

Malia was uneasy entering the town proper this way, via a tiny, narrow road. She couldn't see into the structures, no matter how rundown they were, and to her that posed a potential threat. Anything or anyone could be lurking in the ruins.

Malia scrunched her nose. The salty stench of the ocean, old seaweed, and rotting fish permeated the air, clinging to them and everything around them. She didn't like it.

A small clearing with a statue at its center came into view. Though Malia would have preferred not to take her eyes off her surroundings, she couldn't resist taking a peek at the grayish statue.

It portrayed a tall, muscular man with a slight hunch, a shaggy beard, and beady eyes under strong bushy brows. A peculiar wave of revulsion passed through Malia, who outright loathed those big round pitch-black eyes that seemed to follow her movements. The statue was also covered in seaweed, moss, and bird droppings, the white blotches dripping down its stony surface due to the moisture in the air brought on by the mist.

The glimmering—and oddly squeaky clean—green marble plaque at the base read simply Captain Obed Marsh.

"Do you by any chance know who that is?" Malia asked, hoping Dev had some clue. Though she recognized the alphabet and *could* read, she'd never taken to reading, preferring action over thinking.

Dev looked up at the ugly, rough features of the statue, an expression of disgust on his face as well. "Shay said Marsh was a sea captain from one of the oldest families in the region, and he had a fleet of fishing boats under his command. He was apparently someone important since they erected a statue in his honor."

Malia grimaced. "From the looks of him, I wonder if they did his visage justice."

Dev snorted. "Creepy."

They shared a quiet chuckle under the gloomy skies, which lifted the mood. Some of Malia's unwanted fears evaporated.

Malia moved first, returning to her forward momentum, not wishing to lose daylight over staring at long-ago statues that meant nothing in the here and now. Like spokes on a wheel, several streets veered off from the square, one of them leading to the Old Town Square. They chose Church Street, which after a block would cross Main Street.

Like the gaping mouths and eyes of the dead, the dark windows and shadowy doorways seemed to close in on them. The buildings seemed more intact the deeper they went into the town, suggesting that the harsh weather was blocked by the outer structures, leaving them to take the brunt of heavy storms and snowy winters. With no one left to repair them, the walls of the buildings were cracked or crumbled at the base, and some had started to tilt precariously while others had collapsed.

This is a ghost town, Malia thought. With so many structures exposed to the elements, it was unlikely anything useful would remain. Birds and wild animals would have gotten to the food and other perishables, while clothing and furniture would be mildewed and weatherworn, likely reduced to rags.

For the first time in her life, at least as far back as she could remember, Malia needed to hear a human voice in the unnerving silence. "You and Shay have spoken much about this place and this mission, then?"

In the stillness, she could practically hear Dev gulp. Finally he spoke, his tone low and hesitant. "Shay might be the learned leader of these expeditions, but I'm the captain of the ship. I need to be prepared for anything. Good background information helps."

That wasn't what Malia had been referring to. She wasn't blind. She hadn't missed the furtive, longing glances between Dev and Shay, always made when the other wasn't looking. It was at once endearing and annoying. At times she wondered if all men were like this, hedging and uncertain. Malia liked Shay fine, but she wasn't overly attached to him. These days he was a friend, not a lover— hadn't been one for a long time. One day she would have to encourage the two men to act on their obvious feelings for each other.

Perhaps that day was today, here and now.

But she didn't get the chance to say the words before a noise alerted her, grabbing her attention, a small scratching sound that reached her easily in the stillness.

"Shush," she whispered to Dev, crouching, her rifle at the ready. Next to her, Dev did the same, gearing up for trouble. She gave him a nod to move off, and he responded by shifting in a hurry to the other side of the street, into an alcove. Malia snuck into the shadows of a wall and waited for whatever it was in the fog to come to them.

The fog had become thick and heavy, overbearingly damp, and blinding. They had no way of seeing beyond the edge. Malia cursed the inclement weather, gripping her rifle tighter and then releasing the hold because too tight a grip would make her unable to adapt to all manner of looming threats.

The scratching noise changed to a wooden clatter, followed by the padding of feet.

Malia frowned. A lone survivor? Seemed… improbable.

Like silky veils parting to reveal the stage of life, the pearl-gray mist gave shape to a tiny figure, moving sluggishly down the street toward them. Malia held her breath, not wanting to give her position or presence away. Her last indrawn breath reeked of rotting fish, mold, and decay, and she felt like vomiting.

Then she saw her.

It was a little girl, no more than five winters, surely. Barefoot on the cobblestones, she wore a simple dress that once had been white but now was tarnished by dirt, mud, and food smears. Her long black hair flowed down to the hem of her knee-length garment. The strands covered her face. Behind her she dragged a tiny wooden cart with a dirty dolly and fish stacked in a haphazard pile, one on top of another.

Malia stared, wide-eyed and dumbfounded. A child? Here alone? Impossible.

Yet she didn't ease her hold on the rifle—not for a second.

The girl stopped, swaying back and forth slightly, a finger in her mouth. She looked lost, though her face was hidden behind an obscuring veil of black hair.

What's she waiting for? Malia swallowed, not liking this situation one damn bit.

The little girl cocked her head, but her gaze seemed to be directed at the ground and nothing else. Yet Malia couldn't shake the feeling she knew they were there, observing her.

The girl shifted her weight from one foot to the other. Then her low mumbling turned into a clear, cold rhythm as she sang a morbid sea shanty about waking up a drunken whaler, feeding him to hungry rats, shooting him through the heart, and slicing his throat with a rusty cleaver.

Her tiny, yet sharp, voice lingered and echoed in the ruined town, a voice of childhood, innocence, and purity—and yet suggesting nothing of the kind. So far removed from humanity that Malia felt a chill run up and down her spine.

Fear clutched her heart. Fear of the unknown, of something so alien she had no name for it. For the first time in her life, Malia wanted to run, to get away from this girl, this childlike abomination who sang of murder, blood, and death, a twisted nursery rhyme.

What in the name of all that is holy is she waiting for?

Malia listened to the girl's horrid shanty unwillingly. She desired to silence the voice because it was so wholly alien. Nothing about the girl resembled the kinds of people Malia had come to know since the Cataclysm—people of flesh and blood, emotion and sympathy, heart and kindness. This little child felt devoid of all those warm touches of humanity.

Why does she continue? It's almost as if... she knows we're here....

In the blink of an eye epiphany stirred Malia into motion. She reacted on pure instinct.

The girl's a decoy, a distraction, a lure!

Hairs on the back of her neck stood on end, and Malia spun around as fast as a tornado, her rifle raised, every instinct in her crying out.

The filthy odors of unkempt men of the sea, along with something rotten, filled her nostrils as three men appeared out of the fog like ghosts suddenly taking shape. Malia didn't get a chance to call out to Dev as a smelly rag was shoved against her nose and mouth with steel-like strength. Someone yanked her rifle from her hands and twisted them behind her back.

Whoever these malodorous strangers were, they knew how to work in unison, their efforts coordinated and precise. Malia's head was swimming in the vomit-inducing cloud of fumes that clung to the rag. Her addled brain suspected it was a narcotic created from substances found in the sea.

She struggled fiercely to regain her freedom, but she had no room to maneuver. Her vision blurred as the stunning agent pressed against her face sent her reeling. Her hands were bound with a harsh rope that scratched her skin to blisters, and she was unceremoniously hoisted over a man's shoulder like a lump of cloth. Her abductor's gait was unsteady, as though he had a limp, and his shoulder was oddly shaped, bumpy and swollen.

No sounds emerged when a panel in the wooden wall, where she had hidden mere moments ago, slid open. A biting, sickening breeze blasted against her from the opening as she blinked hard, trying to peer into the darkness below. Though the place stank and made her eyes water, she was able to discern a narrow stone staircase, slimy and grimy and covered with cobwebs and moss, descending down into pitch-black emptiness.

One of the men behind her grunted, and then Malia felt a sharp jolt of pain when he hit her in the back of her head with something thick and blunt. Pain sliced through her for an instant until a merciful darkness bid her entry.

CHAPTER 4

D**EV FROWNED**, puzzled, as he stared at the weird girl. He'd hoped they'd find survivors. And yet… when he looked at the peculiar little thing, bile rose in his throat and shivers ran up and down his spine. There was no chance he'd go and speak with her. Her creepy sea shanty only exacerbated his nerves.

Her long black hair appeared wet, clinging to her skin, veiling her face. Her skin was pale, clammy, and had a sickly green hue. It was autumn, and she wore no shoes, just a thin and dirty summer dress, once white, perhaps, but now gray and filthy. But no matter how infantile she appeared, Dev was as sure as the grave that she was no ordinary little girl and that she didn't need saving.

All of a sudden, the girl stopped singing and swaying and straightened her head from its almost unnatural angle. Then she twirled around and walked slowly back the way she came until she vanished into the fog.

Dev waited in place for several long seconds, waiting for warmth to return to his heart and limbs. Until that moment he hadn't realized how chilled he had become as a result of her presence.

By then the fog was a thick, gray wall. Nothing of the other side of the street remained visible. Dev couldn't hear the padding of her feet or the clanking of her wooden toy anymore, so he assumed it was safe to come out of hiding.

"Malia? The girl's gone," he hissed loudly. No reply came, and Dev began to worry. "Malia? Answer me. Where are you?"

Dev snuck out from the crevice of a broken wall where he'd been hiding, crouched slightly, and skulked across the street toward where he had last seen Malia. He stopped every two steps to listen for anyone approaching. Only silence greeted him. Crumbs from broken pebbles scraped beneath his shoes, and he cringed at the gritty noise every time.

When Dev reached the cracked wall of the building opposite, it was clear Malia wasn't there. Dev spun around, panic starting to take hold of him. "Malia? Where are you? Talk to me." His stage whispers went unanswered. Apart from the fog, nothing moved, and all was silent. As he moved quietly and quickly about, something cracked under his foot. He knelt and took the little object in hand.

It was a small burgundy-colored button from Malia's armored corset, a loose thread still clinging to it.

Closing his eyes briefly and taking a couple fortifying breaths, Dev collected himself. There could be a million reasons why Malia had abandoned her hideout. Someone Dev had not seen because of the mist could have found her post, forcing her to abandon it. If so, all he had to do was wait.

But… though Dev told himself caution might have been Malia's intent, in his heart he knew better. She would not have left without informing him in some fashion. And the torn button spoke of a physical encounter, perhaps a scuffle or an ambush.

So the only possibility left was intervention by parties unknown.

That suggested Dev should make a hasty retreat back to the airship, or risk both Malia and him going missing. And that in turn would ensure Shay, Stork, and even Wren would come after them in the hopes of finding them alive and unharmed. Which would lead them to their doom as well, and Dev couldn't allow that to happen.

Cursing under his breath and vowing to come back for Malia, Dev broke into a run, back the way he came, all the way to the wharf, the coastal road, and finally to the lighthouse. He grabbed the rope, not wanting to waste time waiting for the rope ladder to be lowered. Then he yanked the anchoring knot open and pulled on the rope three times in rapid succession as a sign of danger. Almost immediately someone turned the winch, and Dev rose with the retractable line.

The moment the rope reached the flank of the ship, he gripped the railing and jumped over it. No longer anchored, the skyship creaked in the wind as it slowly glided away. With the engines dampered and the propellers barely turning, the ship would continue to drift a bit, but that could be corrected later. Dev had more critical issues to deal with now.

Stork was manning the winch. The tall, stout hulk of a man must have seen well over fifty winters in his lifetime, but he was still in his prime. His gray-white hair stood up on end, hinting at how much time he spent asleep in his bunk, but his wrinkled, sun-kissed skin spoke of time spent outdoors too. The only thing he had in common with his namesake bird was a long beak.

He scratched at his wiry white beard, scowling at Dev. He didn't deal well with surprises. "What's the rush, boy?" His whiskey-sour voice rang over Dev's gasps as Dev strove to catch his breath after his sprint across the ghost town. Stork didn't enunciate clearly since he had relearned speech relatively late in life. This bothered him greatly and gave him a gruff demeanor at all times.

Shay burst out of the cabin, obviously having heard Dev climb back onboard, and he rushed to Dev and grabbed him, a frantic look in his widened eyes. "What's happened? Where's Malia?"

Dev gripped Shay's shoulders in turn and forced the young scholar to look at him. "That town isn't empty," he explained. "Malia and I saw a young girl there. But… it was wrong. Somehow it was… all wrong." Dev shook his head, trying to make sense of it all. "She just stood there, smack in the middle of the street, singing."

Shay appeared as perplexed as Dev felt. "Singing?"

Now Dev understood. All he had needed was some downtime to gather his thoughts and calm his frayed nerves. "I think she was a distraction." He locked gazes with Shay, who, judging from the look of him, was starting to put the pieces together. "By the time the girl vanished into the fog, Malia was gone. All I found was this." He gave Shay the button, now cracked in the middle as a result of his having stepped on it.

Shay drew in a sharp breath and blinked, eyes glistening with unshed tears. "It's Malia's…."

Dev nodded. "I figured."

Stork came to stand close to them, peering over their shoulders at the button, his expression as wary and furious as Dev's mood. "So… the lass has been taken. What now, Cap?"

Dev didn't leave people behind. "We go down there and we find her."

It didn't take them long to prepare a heavily equipped landing party of three.

Armed to the teeth and ready to take on the world if need be, Dev stood by the bow, weighing their options. Daylight was diminishing as the afternoon waned. It was overcast up here and foggy down below. Neither the time nor the weather were doing them any favors.

Shay moved to his side and stared down at the dark town, where nothing stirred and no lights burned. Dev felt him tremble. "We will find her. Won't we, Dev?"

Dev did what a good captain needed to do—showed unshakable faith in their capabilities. "Yes, we will. Even if we have to burn this place to the ground."

Shay leaned into him slightly, looking sad. Dev wanted to wrap his arm around Shay's shoulder but didn't dare. Shay's beloved was missing, and the overfamiliar gesture would have been inappropriate even if she hadn't been.

Dev was about to step back to put some distance between them when Shay pressed up against him and wound his arms around Dev's waist. "Sorry, Captain," Shay murmured. "I needed a hug, is all."

Closing his eyes, Dev embraced Shay in return. The young scholar's hair smelled of frosty winds, but his skin emanated warmth. Dev wished he could hold Shay like this for the rest of his life. The knowledge that Shay couldn't fill that role for him made Dev sad, longing for Shay to be his to love and be loved by.

So neither of them would forget their duty, Dev whispered, "We will find Malia. This town isn't big enough to hide her from us. I'll get her back to you, Shay. I promise."

Shay stiffened in his arms instantly, and then he moved off, his head bowed, concealing his expressive face from Dev behind a veil of hair. "Yes. Yes, of course." He turned away, staring down into the bleak, dark town. "I have every faith in you, Captain."

Dev swallowed hard, sensing he had disappointed Shay somehow in his attempt to act gallant. But it was too much to hope for that Shay would feel the same. He cleared his throat. "You have everything you need? We won't come back for supplies until nightfall or until we find Malia."

Shay nodded, his voice clipped. "I know." He hesitated, as though he had something on his mind. But then he shook his head and rushed to the cabin door, vanishing inside.

Dev sighed. He hated being in this situation, caught between wanting to be in Shay's company as long as he possibly could and needing to let go of his impossible dream and move on with his life. His emotions couldn't be allowed to interfere with him doing his job to the best of his abilities and to his own satisfaction.

Wren came toward him then, holding a wooly cap in his hands. The short, thin, awkward teenager had come along on this expedition hoping to find those his own age and learn the ins and outs of piloting an airship at the same time. He had proved to be a quick study. Now that it seemed Innsmouth was either deserted or harboring unseen dangers, Dev had decided Wren should stay onboard.

Dev faced the boy. "Wren, remember to coil the rope back up as soon as Shay, Stork, and I are firmly on the ground. But keep the rope ladder ready for quick deployment in case we come back in a hurry."

He knew he didn't really need to repeat his instructions to Wren yet again, but in his heart he needed to emphasize the importance of the boy taking the airship and leaving if it appeared none of them would be coming back alive. Wren would then be the only one left to report back to Canal City about the perils of Innsmouth.

Though he was only fifteen winters old, Wren had a steady head on his shoulders, and once he received orders from his captain, he wouldn't hesitate to execute them—even if that meant abandoning his comrades to certain death. Someone had to survive.

"Yes, Cap." Wren worried his lower lip. "You planning on not coming back?"

Dev chuckled at Wren's challenging, squeaky tone and mild glare. "Don't be silly. We're coming back. All of us together."

Wren stared at him grudgingly but always with awe too. The boy was a head shorter than Dev, who felt protective of the awkward teenager. His copper-colored hair shone whenever the sun deemed fit to show its radiant face through the barely parting dark blue clouds, which was a rare occurrence indeed. His green eyes, freckles, and upturned nose gave him a haughty expression, though he was sweet and down-to-earth. His clothes—dark pants, heavy boots, white dress shirt with the sleeves rolled up, an open vest, and a burgundy cap now back on his head—always seemed to drown him under their weight, giving him the look of a boy trying on his father's clothes.

But the school of life had taught the whole world. Wren might have been fifteen, but he was going on thirty. Wren was like Dev in many ways. They'd both had to fight to survive, but thankfully, only Dev had the scars to prove it. Wren had been spared the worst life could throw at you, having been born in the safe haven of Canal City.

"Don't dillydally," Wren told Dev, who smiled at the order made in earnest. That was one of Wren's favorite words, perhaps recently learned, judging by how often he used it. "If you're not back or haven't sent me a message by moonrise, I'm leaving."

Dev nodded firmly. "Good boy." He might have ruffled the boy's hair had he not worn his cap—which he wore specifically to avoid being treated like a boy. He was young, but he had a grown man's pride. Dev had to respect that if he wanted Wren's respect returned. "If Malia comes back before us, somehow, wait for us."

Wren frowned, glancing over his shoulder to see if Shay had returned, which he hadn't. "She's a warrior, to be sure, but…. You think that's likely?"

Dev breathed in and out a couple of times, hedging. In the end he went with the truth. "I hope so. I really do."

"Was Wren upset he couldn't come with us?" Shay asked quietly as he, Dev, and Stork walked around the harbor bay toward town. He quickly glanced back at the airship. After retrieving the rope, Wren had adjusted the engines to increase the speed of the propellers enough to keep the unanchored ship in relatively the same position.

Dev shrugged. "We need someone onboard in case Malia comes back on her own, or if we need to make a quick getaway. Wren has no experience with weapons or combat, so he was the natural choice. He understands his duty." Dev wasn't willing to entertain the idea of bringing everyone to the ground for a search party even if Wren had thrown a teenage temper tantrum. Thankfully, he hadn't.

Foul odors of decay and rot permeated the very air they breathed and clung to their attire and to the ruined, collapsed buildings of the town. The water level must have risen and gone down with the tide, since salty lines on the buildings' walls showed how high the tide had reached. Beyond the town, where structures grew scarce, birches shone with fall colors, adding a few much-needed specks of color to the otherwise drab, gloomy surroundings.

As they came up to the junction where Water Street joined Eliot Street, Dev hesitated, stopping dead in his tracks. His past actions haunted him. He'd lost a valuable, respected comrade-in-arms. A part of him wished desperately to turn back and sail off into the sunset on the airship, forgetting he had ever laid eyes on this dismal place.

Shay touched his arm gently. "Is that the way you went before?"

Dev nodded, tongue glued to his palate, not knowing whether to shiver, vomit, or fire his gun just to scare the shadows into movement.

"Should we retrace your steps or choose another route? Perhaps if we searched different areas—"

"No!" Dev didn't shout, but his voice was as adamant as his will. "We're *not* going to get separated. We're going to stick together, no matter what." *I'm not losing anyone else.* But Dev wisely left that unsaid as it would have been unduly emotional commentary. He needed to maintain his strong appearance as captain of this desolate expedition.

"Which way should we go, then?" Shay frowned, and Dev knew he was irritated, a bit at least, at Dev's behavior. Dev could relate. He wanted to find Malia too, only for different reasons. She wasn't Dev's woman, but she could hold her own in a fight, and Dev was absolutely certain they would end up needing a gunslinger before their expedition was at an end, not to mention the wider efforts of rebuilding their world.

Dev pointed forward. "Let's go to Dock Street or River Road, or whatever it's called. It follows the Manuxet River and gives us a better vantage point on the town around us."

"There are several falls where the river cascades down the hillside," Shay said, his tone hinting at his reticence. "With the noise, we won't be able to hear much."

Dev had considered that. He hoped the fog would have lifted around the river, giving them better visibility. If someone did try to ambush or attack them, they could jump into the water and let it carry them back out to the harbor. If they then kept up a good swimming pace, they'd reach their ship sooner than anyone else. *If we don't drown first, that is.*

Shay waved a hand about without waiting for a response. "Never mind. You're in charge, Dev. I trust your judgment. Let's follow the river." He traced the route with his gaze, obviously going over the maps in his head. "We should at least check out Federal Street. That's the main thoroughfare of the town, with many main buildings along the way. It connects Church Green Plaza and the New Town Square too. The town hall, several churches, public library, and schools are close to the Church Green, and the bank, grocery stores, and fishing fleet offices are around the New Town Square. All well worth a look."

As usual, Dev was struck with awe at his adventurous companion's deep dedication and wealth of knowledge. "Okay. Let's find this Federal Street first." He glanced around warily and lowered his voice to a near whisper. "Just remember there's at least one person living here that we know of. She couldn't have survived here on her own, so expect the unexpected." Addressing both Shay and Stork, Dev needed to impress upon them the importance of keeping alert, with a healthy dose of suspicion.

Stork said nothing, merely nodded. Shay offered an encouraging smile, though some anxiety clearly lay buried beneath the surface. That was enough to assure Dev he'd gotten his message across.

With Dev in the lead, Stork guarding the rear, and Shay between them, the party walked to the first bridge closest to the harbor and the sea. The wood had rotted through, and many planks looked loose or about to break at the first rough wave slamming against them.

The Manuxet River wove through Innsmouth like a sea serpent, with rocky rapids and four steeper waterfalls before it reached the harbor inlet. Dev stared—again—at the dark, misty town towering above them, rising up the hillside. The same fear that had gripped him before did so again. The buildings, all of them partially collapsed, in ruins, seemed to teeter precariously, as if ready to break down and crash on top of them at any minute.

Dev discarded these worries. Though potentially valuable as warning against impending calamities, they would prove paralyzing if he heeded them. Malia would not be found if Dev was squeamish.

Like a death shroud, the gray fog rolled down the hillside, as if conjured up by their unseen enemies to prevent them from finding their fallen comrade. Dev hated the mist, how it obscured their view. But… he'd been right too. The mist appeared to draw back from the river, which did give them an edge when it came to visibility.

"Stay close and look sharp," Dev ordered one final time before they began their ascent of Dock Street.

The town rose on their right, looming over them, watching them through dark broken windows and black doorways. The odors of sea salt and fish in every stage of decomposition filled the air with an invisible, noxious fume. Dev grimaced. He focused on breathing through his mouth, but soon found that left a bitter, nauseous coating on his tongue.

"I know this is a seaport, but really…." Shay's whisper told Dev that he too found their surroundings almost unbearable to his senses.

"We just passed a fish-packing house," Dev replied, speaking softly and slowly to ensure he could hear if someone—or something— approached.

Though their newfound society had learned a great many things since the Cataclysm, superstition ran amok. They had virtually no way of telling if a threat was likely, possible, or impossible. Factual knowledge was a hard commodity to come by these days. Monsters existed in the frightened, ignorant minds of many post-Cataclysm survivors. As usual, the only cure for those paranoid thoughts was a proper education.

Dev really wished they could remember if their fears were warranted or not.

The river ran unobstructed on their left. Yet the flow proceeded sluggishly, like half of it were barely churning mud, and the surface rippled as if brushed by a breeze—though there was none to speak of. The next wooden bridge they encountered was broken, with a few shattered planks still clinging to the intact portions by twisted nails, dangling like wooden offerings to the water.

Crumbled shacks and tiny cabins lay on the sloping riverside, all of them utter ruins, tilted toward the water or halfway descended into the depths. On their left, no structures remained standing.

Except for one. The crooked, formerly white, sign above the wide-open double doors read Marsh Refinery. The building looked like a warehouse, with huge doors, whitewashed walls—though now in far less than pristine condition—and a slanted steel roof, gone mostly green in color. Inside they could see the shadowy shapes of metal pillars and struts, along with big boxes. Inoperative machines must be farther inside, hidden from any clear line of sight.

"That was the main operation in this town?" Dev asked, taking a glimpse at the place but still keeping an eye on the rest of the town, searching for stealthy movements and unnatural sounds.

Shay nodded. He looked pale and hesitant, if not outright scared. His gaze swept the building like he was taking in every detail, for who knew what purpose. "The fishing industry was key here. When ill fortune out at sea and numerous shipwrecks caused trade with the South Seas to dwindle, the town started to die. But they had a lucky windfall—a surprising amount of fish and other catch seemed to appear out of thin air. Captain Obed Marsh, who brought some kind of a sea-creature cult from the Pacific Ocean into town, took advantage of the fortuitous occurrence with his own shipping fleet, and so Innsmouth became a boomtown. That was how the people were able to save the industry and their town. Newfound gold made the townsfolk rich. At least until a mysterious plague came...." He seemed to have more to say, his mouth opening and closing, but he kept frowning and staring about uncertainly.

Dev wanted to calm him, so he rested a hand on Shay's shoulder. Shay jumped, clearly startled by the sudden physical contact. He laughed anxiously. "Sorry. I'm just... nervous, I guess." He swallowed, and Dev could relate. He felt off kilter as well.

"Come on. Federal Street is just up ahead." Dev wanted to sound confident, strong in leadership skills, and powerful, as though there was nothing to worry about. Yet while his voice didn't strain, he was surely straining the truth a bit.

The three of them started moving again.

A few wilted plants, dried-up grasses, and barren trees grew on the riverside, but none of them appeared verdant or vibrant. They were as lifeless as the town appeared to be, mere husks of their former natural glory.

The gravelly pavement scrunched under their feet, broadcasting their position to anyone who might be listening. Dev cringed with every step, no matter how softly he trod.

As they reached Federal Street, they stepped onto deteriorating asphalt, cracked and broken in many places, with brownish plants wedged in the cracks. It was easy to see that this was the most important and well-used route in town because it was wider than Dock Street, obviously allowing for both two-way traffic and sidewalks.

"So which way?" Dev looked in both directions. The street occupied roughly the same elevation on both sides of the river, so both ways looked the same.

Shay worried his bottom lip, he too looking both ways with sharply assessing eyes. "The town hall and other places for public assembly, including the library and schools, are mostly to the north. Places where you can get food, drink, shelter, and medications are to the south, across the river. But... the four maps I have show subtle differences, so...." He locked gazes with Dev and shrugged. "Both directions are equally possible when it comes to both survivors and information. Your call, Captain."

CHAPTER 5

SHAY LOVED the decisive look on Dev's face. When contemplative, he seemed infinitely wise. The fact that Shay took the time to notice Dev's good looks when he should have been worrying about Malia's well-being made him feel like a heel.

Dev rubbed his jaw, the beard bristles creating a scratchy sound. "Our primary task is to find accurate factual information to aid us in finding Malia. Survivors are a bonus, but after all this time…. We go to the library. If there are people left here who can tell us what we need to know, they'll be near or at the place where knowledge is stored."

Shay nodded in agreement, while Stork's nod signaled resolute obedience.

Resuming their former positions in their procession, they walked north. Shay knew not to speak unless asked. Dev would be scouring the path ahead with all his senses, and he needed his wits about him. He would have seen the same maps as Shay and therefore knew that up ahead would be New Church Green, a circular plaza with holy buildings for a variety of religions. If Dev needed to ascertain more, he would simply ask Shay.

Sometimes Shay was certain Dev asked him questions just to hear Shay's voice.

That was what Shay chose to believe, anyway.

After they had walked forward a block, flanked by rundown buildings with torn drapes flapping in broken windows and empty doorways like toothless mouths, the ring-shaped plaza came into view, dominating the crossroads of Federal Street and Church Street.

It was easy to see why it was referred to as the Green. A street circled a lawn that had once undoubtedly been green. Now the only flecks of color were the sickly gray-green moss and the fallen red, yellow, and brown autumn leaves. The grass was either dried and dead or covered by a muddy ooze spread around in tiny puddles.

What was different from the rest of the town they'd seen so far was the state of the buildings around the plaza. They appeared to be in much fairer condition. The walls had cracks, but at least they stood firm in place. The curtained windows weren't broken, and faint glows flickered inside, like distant stars dancing. The doors were closed rather than tilted on rusty hinges or forced open by nature or the hands of men. No voices, no whispers, no music, no song—nothing man-made was audible, and yet it was evident these structures were currently lived in.

Though excited at the prospect of possibly finding survivors, Shay shivered. After all, Malia was still missing, and whoever dwelled in this town that time had forgotten, they had snatched her—a seasoned warrior—with ease.

"In olden times, at least according to some of the books I've read, people sought refuge or sanctuary on hallowed ground, such as churches." Shay offered this piece of information even though no one had asked. He just wanted to hear a familiar voice, and even his own would do in a pinch.

Dev nodded grimly to show he'd heard. But judging from his stark expression, Shay had a sneaking suspicion Dev wasn't sold on the idea that people might have chosen this town as any kind of refuge from the wilderness—or from whatever.

"What's that?" With the barrel of his rifle, Dev pointed at the biggest building, the one on the west side of the plaza. The hewn walls stood black, with shimmers of green, as if serving as a warning to onlookers to find respite elsewhere. The sense of the place was foreboding indeed, and Shay swallowed hard, uncomfortable simply staring at the structure.

Shay pointed at the sign above the arched doorway. "That plaque says it's the Esoteric Order of Dagon." The black stone of the heavy-looking plaque glimmered, and the green letters did the same. "Why?" Shay continued, even though he was reasonably sure Dev must have felt a similar sinister air emanating from the whole structure.

Dev snorted quietly. "'Cause I've never heard of Dagon. That's why."

Shay had to chuckle at the man's cynical, yet amused, tone. "Well, I think it's probably a lodge or a chapter house for some kind of fraternal organization, like a craft guild or a religious sect. Dagon could be a fancy title for the chapter house's leader or perhaps the name for the deity they worship."

"Uh-huh." Dev scanned the windows and doorways with a critical eye. "You mean the weird faith Obed Marsh brought back from the Pacific?"

"Possibly. The books I read about Marsh were told in journal form by outsiders, so what little information there was, it was mostly hearsay, rumors, and tall tales." Shay worried his bottom lip. An instinctive sense of dread grew in him. He wanted to leave. His legs felt like jelly, ready to cave from under him at any moment. But Shay was loyal to a fault. He refused to believe Malia could already be dead. He would be brave for her—and for Dev too. Glancing at the man in question, Shay suppressed a deep sigh of longing. He desperately wanted to feel Dev's arms around him, offering him comfort and unconditional love.

"Assuming Dagon refers to a figure of religious significance, what do you know about this Dagon and his followers?" Judging from his question, Dev clearly was trying to decide on the best course of action and required as many facts as he could muster.

"I don't know much, I'm afraid," Shay replied hesitantly, not wanting to give misleading or faulty information. That type of blunder could jeopardize their mission and endanger their very lives. "I believe he's a fertility god, associated with fish and fishing. I can't remember where or when he was initially worshiped, but based on Marsh's story, the origin of the faith could be somewhere in the Pacific. Sorry I don't have more to give you."

Dev glanced at Shay over his shoulder and smiled reassuringly. "That's still more than either of us know." He gestured between himself and Stork, who seemed remarkably unfazed by the subject or their surroundings. Shay thought that might be because in many ways Stork was too ignorant to understand the threats they were facing and therefore knew no fear. Immediately he felt guilty and ashamed for thinking of his comrade in such a fashion, and he bowed his head to hide his undoubtedly flaming cheeks.

To get his wayward emotions under control, Shay veered the conversation onto a new topic. "What's your plan?"

Dev didn't answer for a long while. Finally he sighed. "We're going in."

Naturally the door creaked sharply as Dev pushed it open. Anyone within a mile was sure to have heard them enter.

Shay cringed and cursed under his breath. *Too late now.* The die was cast; their ultimate fate the final bet.

With somewhat foolhardy determination, they snuck in stealthily.

The lobby had once been luxurious to the point of pretentious. Two sets of stairs, one on either side, framed the round room. But the once lush red rugs had vermin-devoured holes in them, and dust covered them like a second gray carpet. The wood-paneled walls might have been shiny and dark as a sign of prestige in times past, but now planks were missing or broken. Similarly, many of the spindles of the stair railings were splintered or simply gone. A huge grandfather clock stood by the staircase, the thick glass covering the dead clock face covered in cobweb-like patterns where it had been smashed but not entirely broken. A white sheet, now in tatters, covered the twisted chandelier, most of its crystals in shards on the floor beneath it. Eroded rectangles on the walls showed where paintings had once hung, and pieces of broken vases lay scattered around the lobby. *No one here to clean up the mess*, Shay thought, shivering.

"Stay close," Dev whispered harshly, betraying his concern. Tight quarters made for a lot of opportunities for things to go horribly wrong. "No one goes anywhere alone."

To the left and right of the lobby were two lounges or waiting areas, and these they explored briefly. Huge fireplaces, cold and filled with ashes, dominated wide spaces occupied by couches and armchairs, credenzas and bookshelves, liquor cabinets and bar carts.

All of them were ransacked and empty, destroyed or chopped into pieces. Nothing of the rooms' former glory remained.

Back in the two-story lobby, Dev pointed the barrel of his rifle to a dark set of double doors hanging askew opposite the main entrance. "No jumping at shadows," Dev instructed.

Shay agreed. Bullets were scarce, and if anyone still lived here, there was no point in scaring them away with an apparent gunfight. During his first expedition, Shay had wasted two good bullets shooting at a mirror. Better safe than sorry, of course, but that mistake still annoyed him.

Dev first and Stork last, the three men entered the dark corridor beyond the doors.

Even with all his precautions and winters' worth of battle experience, Shay still wasn't adequately prepared for the unusual and frightening sight that awaited them.

No candles or gaslights lit the stark interiors, far removed from the luxury of the lobby and the two lounges. Claustrophobic, narrow hallways, sunken ceilings, moldy carpets, tilting walls with peeling wallpaper that bared stone and wooden structures, and rooms empty of furniture all stared back at them with hollow eyes. One might have rightly assumed the place was as unlived-in as the vast majority of towns in the world today.

Except… they weren't alone.

Men, women, and children, all quiet as the grave, shifted silently in the shadows, clumsily lurking from one room to the next. Some stopped and stared at the newcomers, but their gazes were empty and void. Most took one look at them and, as if seeing right through them, went on in their hulking gaits, indifferent and uncomprehending.

Shay grew certain the Cataclysm had hit this town hard, leaving behind nothing but hollow shells of people who were mindless, speechless, and could offer no aid to them in their mission.

And yet, the men, women, and children Shay saw looked and felt… off. More off than the aftereffects of the Cataclysm could account for. Nothing about them seemed familiar. Huddled in small groups, they said and did nothing but stare at Shay, Dev, and Stork as they wandered past. No emotions were reflected on their inanimate, almost lifeless, faces. They appeared completely devoid of that elusive spark of human spirit.

While the children appeared relatively normal, despite their unkempt appearance and odd clothing, on closer inspection the adults veered far from the image of humanity as Shay knew it. They seemed to lack ears and noses, or perhaps these features were simply sunken deep into their bodies due to deficiencies brought on by lack of proper diet and clean water. Their skin looked blue or gray and scaly, with odd-shaped blotches of white or green, all of which gleamed as though moist, wet, or rubbery. Only a few of the children had hair; the adults had none.

The worst, however, was their eyes. Huge, much bigger than a normal human's, their eyes appeared almost completely black and were bulging and glassy. Was Shay seeing right? Did those eyes appear closer to the sides of their faces than normal? And they never seemed to blink.

Shay didn't know whether to run down the street, swept up in waves of madness, or to stay and ogle these strange beings who from afar might have been mistaken for humans, but not up close. These folks were the epitome of abnormality. In any other circumstances, Shay would have rejoiced at finding survivors. But now all he wanted to do was fly away and forget he had ever seen these freaks of nature.

Surely all this could not have happened in a mere twenty-odd winters? Evolution didn't happen so fast, did it? Shay shuddered at the mere sight of the townsfolk of Innsmouth, Massachusetts. The instinct of flight kicked in with a vengeance, and his feet all but turned back the way he came without his volition.

A shuffling sound served as the only warning of the arrival of a man who seemed to be in charge. The others stepped back, giving the man a wide berth. With tiny, slow steps, the old, gray man approached, his upper back hunched, his body covered with what looked like a plain, dirty bathrobe. His skin, thin as paper, seemed ready to crack and tear at a moment's notice.

His appearance didn't match those of the others. Yet his neck and hands displayed the same grayish scales as the rest. But he blinked, and his blue eyes were a normal size and shape.

"Greetings, fellow travelers," the man said in a thin, fluty, slightly irritating voice. "I am Doctor Lethe. Welcome to Innsmouth."

Shay started at the man's speech patterns. There was no fumbling for the right words, no hesitation in enunciation, no sign of any inability to voice his thoughts. Shay was a scholar, and even he had trouble sometimes. But not this man.

"Hello," Shay said politely, offering a smile he knew was tight and insecure. Doctor Lethe bowed his head infinitesimally. "I am Shay. These are my companions, Dev and Stork." The old man smiled at them as well, a tiny nod of acknowledgment. "This might sound strange, but we have come here to… rescue you."

The old man laughed, a tenuous and whiny sound high in his throat. "I thank you for coming all this way to offer help, gentlemen, but I assure you, we require none." He spread his arms in invitation. "If anything, we can aid *you*."

SHAY EXCHANGED glances with Dev. "I'm s-sorry. I don't quite understand."

Doctor Lethe swished his hand in a beckoning gesture, his shoulder-length gray hair swaying about him. "Please, come with me, and all shall be explained." He shambled toward another door at the end of the hallway and pushed it open with a jarring creak.

As the three men followed, Dev asked, "How many of you are there in here?"

Doctor Lethe shrugged. "A few. Enough."

Shay saw Dev frown at the vague response and stepped in. "This is incredible. How have you been able to survive all this time?"

Doctor Lethe offered a faint lopsided smile over his shoulder. "We manage."

It was Shay's turn to feel suspicious of the circumspect answers that gave him nothing to work with. "So you have supplies and resources available? Like fresh drinking water, fresh food, adequate clothing for the seasons and the weather?"

Doctor Lethe nodded. "Yes." He gestured for them to enter a shaded room as large as the lobby, with heavy red drapes covering the windows.

Dev pointed at the large fireplace on their right, shivering. "It's chilly in here. Could we maybe light a fire?" He probably would have hugged himself if he hadn't been holding a rifle in his hands, Shay assumed.

With a quick shake of his head, Doctor Lethe gave them a twisted smile, almost a cringe. "I'm afraid the chimney's been blocked off. Smoke and light from fires tend to lure the scavengers and bandits from the wilderness, so we try not to use them. And," he added, with a lick of his lips, "we prefer to eat our food raw."

Shay grimaced inwardly. Uncooked food? Surely that couldn't be healthy in the long run? One couldn't eat raw fish and meat daily without getting scurvy or some other debilitating vitamin deficiency. He quivered at the mere notion. Then again, these people did feel... wrong.

He decided to steer the conversation back on track. "We come from Canal City. It's south of here. We came to offer you a chance to get rescued."

Doctor Lethe waved his hands about, seemingly content and dismissive. "We are not in need of rescue, as noble as the sentiment may be."

Shay had his doubts, but he also had to accept the possibility these people might be disinclined to leave their home. Even if they couldn't remember it. "But you're awfully close to the new wilderness. You'd be safer with us in Canal City."

"Thank you, Shay," Doctor Lethe said with a courteous bow. "But no, thank you. We have no wish to leave Innsmouth." He flashed a toothy grin with grayish, sharp teeth, some missing. "Perhaps you and your people would consider coming to live with us here."

Shay swallowed suddenly rising bile. "T-thank you kindly, b-but no. Canal City is big and offers us greater protection against the wilderness."

The old man quirked an eyebrow. "You must be running low on provisions and other resources by now, if you insist on huddling together in a broken-down major town."

Shay glanced at Dev who, like him, was immediately on guard. Shay understood. How could this man know anything about a city he'd never seen? How could he know squat about machines and equipment that no longer functioned? Something smelled fishy in the small town of Innsmouth, Massachusetts.

"We manage," Shay replied, offering his most sincere smile, though he was nothing of the kind. "Do you by any chance have any supplies, provisions, medicines, or books to spare?"

Doctor Lethe laughed, a hollow, scratchy sound that bounced off the walls, and echoed through the building. "Oh, we can do much better than that, gentlemen."

"Oh?" Shay went for nonchalance, but he had a bad feeling. He inched closer to Dev without conscious thought until he felt Dev do the same. Their arms brushed, and Shay felt instantly calmer.

This time, Doctor Lethe's widening grin hit Shay with a chill of foreboding. *Danger*, his every instinct shouted. Shay had no idea what to expect. The old man's thin voice had dropped to a tone both throaty and husky, as though serving up a warning of something ominous about to take place.

"From your childhood to this very day," Doctor Lethe said, "we can restore all your memories, full and intact, with not a single cherished moment or treasured sensation lost."

CHAPTER 6

MALIA GROANED as she regained consciousness. The surface she lay upon was soft and puffy, like a billowy cloud. Her body warm and her mind hazy, she didn't wish to move but knew she had to.

"You're awake. Good."

Malia started at the deep, masculine voice somewhere close-by. The low purr echoed around, giving Malia simultaneous goose bumps from chills and hot flashes. She tried to open her eyes to see and her mouth to speak, but an odd lassitude kept her prisoner.

"You're safe here. So be calm."

Blinking at last, Malia tried to get a read on her surroundings. But her vision remained foggy. The only thing she managed to discern was the baldachin bed she was lying in. Its thick brown velvet drapes were drawn aside. The heated comforter invited Malia to sink into the softness and enjoy a touch of luxury. Airship bunks were nothing like this, since they hugged the metal walls of the hull.

"I apologize for your rough treatment earlier. My men can be somewhat overzealous in their interpretation of my commands."

This time Malia made a serious attempt to wake up completely. Her bashed skull was throbbing, sending red-hot jolts of pain searing through her head and body whenever she moved an inch. She fought the weariness settling into her bones and muscles and pushed herself into a sitting position.

The room was dimly lit, so at least sharp lights weren't adding to her discomfort. Apart from the bed, there seemed to be no furnishings. Only faint, shadowy shapes appeared here and there, and she couldn't tell if they were cloth-covered furniture or just plain shadows.

"Here's something to drink. The nausea and pain will subside."

A huge hand with a dark-grayish complexion and no body hairs offered her a cup made of metal. As Malia wrapped her shaky hands around it, the hot liquid warmed her hands and soothed her frayed nerves. Not that she would show those vulnerabilities to her… captor? Savior?

Cautiously she sniffed at the substance in the cup. The liquid sloshed about as her hands trembled. A soothing odor of spices—clove, cinnamon, ginger, and cardamom—blackcurrant, rum, raisins, and almonds wafted up to her nose. But her distrust of the stranger who gave her the hot drink had her move the drink down to her lap, untouched.

A deep chuckle echoed in the room. "It isn't poisoned or rancid, I assure you."

With her reservations dampened only slightly, Malia took a small sip.

Instant heat spread through her, and the spices awakened her taste buds. Whatever the fatigue that had plagued her, it vanished into thin air. Malia was wide-awake.

"See? Quite good, isn't it? My followers make the mulled wine themselves."

Malia's gaze traced the path of the voice until she got a good look at its owner.

He was a tall, swarthy man with rugged, handsome features, an engaging smile, and a well-built body. His thick, pitch-black hair was his most defining characteristic, cascading down his back and his sides in long, thin braids. His weather-beaten skin implied an outdoorsy nature, but his huge, glowing dark eyes suggested he belonged to the realm of shadows instead.

Unlike any man Malia had ever met, he was a mystery, and Malia wasn't sure how to take him on.

Once she had shoved herself out of bed, stood, and placed the half-filled drink cup on the bedside table, she began to notice that the state of the bedroom was in fact far from luxurious. The tall windows were boarded, the curtains eaten through by bugs and worms, every nook and cranny was covered in cobwebs, and the place reeked of dust, animal droppings, and age.

"Where am I?" Malia asked warily and refocused on her host. "Who are you?"

The man bowed his head, his long braids framing his face and body like a black veil. "Forgive me. I'm Nicholas. And this rundown mansion once belonged to Captain Obed Marsh. I am his… relative, in a manner of speaking." Nicholas smiled, a joyous and inviting gesture. Yet the dark glow in his eyes overshadowed the expression.

Under the guise of adjusting her attire, Malia made a quick inspection of her concealed weapons. They all seemed to be intact. She wasn't sure how to take that. Either this man's folks were dumb or inefficient—or they'd let her keep her arsenal because they didn't see her as a threat.

"Why did you abduct me?" Malia kept a tight rein over her ire but heard the sharpness in her tone, the demand for answers.

Nicholas shook his head, his smile unwavering. "You misunderstood our meaning. You were brought here for your safety. You are a woman, after all." Malia was about to ask what that comment entailed, but he beat her to it. "Since the Cataclysm, our streets are no strangers to the wildlings, scavengers, and bandits in the vast unknown outside of town. You being a woman would naturally make you their desired target."

Frowning, Malia considered Nicholas's words. They sounded innocent enough, and protective too, but she wasn't the type to fall for a line. "What do you know about the Cataclysm?"

Nicholas quirked an eyebrow. "I know that you and your friends are from Canal City, the place formerly known as New York, that your name is Malia, that you have lost all your past memories, and that you call the event that caused this the Cataclysm. The world has undergone a huge change."

That he knew so much about her raised Malia's suspicion further. She rested a hand over her hidden knife. "Perhaps I wasn't clear. What do *you of Innsmouth* know about the Cataclysm?"

Nicholas chuckled, his amiable expression unchanged. "You are a curious one, aren't you?"

He moved off, turned away, and ambled toward the window, where he shifted a plank to the side with a creak to peer outside. Malia waited, ready to leap into action at a moment's notice.

"The simplest answer?" Nicholas said smoothly. "Here, in Innsmouth, there was no Cataclysm."

THAT REPLY shook Malia to the core. But she struggled not to show even a sliver of her shock. "Explain."

Nicholas swiveled around slowly, revealing only his profile to her. He seemed pensive and lost in thought. "We are not alone here in Innsmouth. There is one who must not be named. He provides for us, though he dreams about us from afar, from the cold heart of infinity."

Malia had no idea what Nicholas was talking about, but she was beginning to doubt the man's sanity. Yet she made no comment, choosing to wait and listen.

"He is abysmal," Nicholas continued, his voice deepening, carrying a darker tone that Malia definitely didn't like. "Deep in unlit chambers beneath the waves, he dwells among the black stars and dreams, for should he awaken, the universe would cease to be."

Malia had had enough. "What does this… being have to do with this town remaining untouched by the Cataclysm?"

Nicholas smiled again, the shadows evaporating from his face. The black glow in his eyes unnerved Malia, who tightened her grip on her knife handle. "He sleeps for us. But his mind, his consciousness and awareness, are not tied to the mortal coil of men. The spark within humans, he does not share it. His vastness is cosmic."

Malia gritted her teeth, her irritation starting to show. She was close to shutting up this raving lunatic with a kiss from her blade. "Your words mean nothing to me. Clearly you are either incapable of or unwilling to assist me. Where are my friends? I want to see them now."

Nicholas chuckled again, the sound a warning of a danger looming ahead. "They are safe, like you. They are speaking with my followers at the Order of Dagon lodge. They are about to be offered the rarest of opportunities, one they cannot and will not refuse." He extended his hand in invitation. "Come with me, and I will take you to them."

Hesitating, Malia stared at the offered hand. A pure instinct screamed at her, and she heeded it. "Lead on." She nodded her head to show him he should go first, with her following in his footsteps.

Nicholas laughed, his head thrown back. "You are a truly suspicious person. I like that about you. Distrust serves you well, I'm sure." He shrugged, never losing his jovial attitude. With a determined stride, he walked to the doorway, once painted red but now flaking, and Malia followed.

Only… where Malia should have been able to see a corridor or stairs or anything familiar, she saw instead a swirling pool of blackness. It shimmered and swelled, moved by forces Malia neither knew nor understood.

"What is that?" She pointed at the doorway, taking a firm step back.

Nicholas glanced at her over his shoulder, his expression arrogant and condescending, even though the ever-present smile never faltered. "It's a portal. It takes you to anywhere you wish in an instant. Only I can travel through it safely. All others will perish. Well, except you."

Malia regarded Nicholas like a doctor might a mental patient, expecting insane ramblings as a normal occurrence. "How does it work?" she asked, deciding to placate the man who had ordered her abduction. Nicholas had shown both regard *and* disregard for her health and safety, and Malia was less than thrilled about either. One of these was a lie. She had a feeling Nicholas had no knowledge of empathy or sympathy; he merely mimicked those emotions to pass as a human being.

Nicholas smirked. "I control the portal with my thoughts. You must hold my hand or risk getting lost in empty star fields of the blackest night."

Once again he extended his hand. Nicholas stared at her daringly, as if expecting her to refuse. She nearly did. Finally, with no small amount of trepidation, she took his hand.

His hand was cool and… moist? It didn't feel like sweat. His skin was slick and scaly to the touch, but Malia abstained from looking down. If she let go of him, there was no telling what would happen or where she would end up.

Like a shadow sliding silently from light to dark, Nicholas strode over the threshold, and Malia followed, pulled into the void.

Instinctively she held her breath and closed her eyes. She feared what she might see and whether she would be able to draw breath. Pressure built around her, squeezing her body from all directions. Yet her body was weightless, as though she were treading tiptoe on clouds and mist. She wondered briefly if she could fly.

But bone-chilling, icy fumes licked at her skin. Wherever she was, it was far removed from any place she had ever been. She desperately needed the trip to end.

She jolted when her next step landed on a wooden floor. The autumn air was still cool but nothing like the freezing steam that had surrounded her a mere moment ago.

Breathing hard, she fought down panic. Soon she calmed and opened her eyes.

They stood in front of another doorway. This time there was no swirling black mass, but a thin foggy veil, slightly obscuring the view but none of the sound.

On the other side, in a large room with a lot of odd-looking people, stood Dev, Shay, and Stork.

MALIA SURGED into movement toward her friends—but the misty veil was an invisible wall. It gave way just enough for Malia not to injure herself. But it didn't allow her to pass through.

Angry, she faced Nicholas, who stood behind her. "Why can't I go to them?"

"You wanted to see them. And now you can."

Malia reached for her blade as she growled, "I want to speak with them. Now."

Nicholas crossed his arms over his chest, appearing pleased with himself, and leaned on the doorframe. "Not yet. Listen, Malia, and hear the offer first. Watch and find out where your friends really stand."

Irritation aside, Malia flinched inwardly. "How do you know my name?"

Nicholas hummed. "I will tell you everything. Soon. Lesson in humanity first." With a smirk, he nodded toward the room they could see into and hear from but not enter.

With worry etched on her brow, Malia observed the happenings in the large room.

A hunchbacked man with gray hair was speaking to Dev, Shay, and Stork. "You do not believe me, I can tell. No matter. I will prove myself to you."

He waved behind him impatiently. A little girl with a half-torn dress and long black hair stepped forward. Malia stiffened. *It's the creepy girl who was singing that bloody sea shanty.* She handed the old man an object shrouded in gray fabric.

"Thank you, Misery," the old man said to the girl, who nodded and ambled back into the shadows.

The old man uncovered the object with great care, handling the item lovingly and with reverence. The object was a huge glowing silver key, the colors shifting from deep blues to sickly greens, and then shimmering to near black. The key seemed to pulsate, its glow brightening and dimming as though it were breathing or contained a beating heart.

All Malia knew was that the thing oozed an unnatural radiance.

"This," the man said solemnly, his crooked fingers caressing the object. His touch left undulations behind, like a fish swimming close to the surface of a pond, rippling the calm waters. "This is the Key of Condensation, the key through the gates of dreams and memories."

"The what?" Dev asked, a baffled expression on his face.

The hunchback gazed at the shimmering object with deep affection and affinity. "The key contains condensed cosmic energy, tightly packed for convenience and efficiency."

"What does it do?" Shay asked, head cocked, brow furrowed. Malia smiled. That was Shay's scholarly look, and it suited him.

"The key retains all the knowledge in the universe within its shining depths. As you touch it, your lost memories will return." Malia wasn't the only one who gasped upon hearing the bold, out-of-this-world statement, uttered with absolute certainty. But she watched the old man's smile grow into an animalistic grin and knew the offer was too good to be true.

"That's incredible," Shay uttered, his voice breathy with astonishment. "The world could heal again." His enthusiasm was boyish and innocent—and impossible in this horrible town. Malia feared for him.

"Yes, indeed." The old man nodded, his grin predatory. "For some."

Shay's smile vanished and was replaced by confusion. But Dev grew tense, and his gaze traveled the room, searching for danger. Malia would have done the same.

"What does that mean, Doctor Lethe?" Shay asked, his befuddlement increasing.

The old man—Doctor Lethe, apparently—feigned nonchalance with a shrug that spoke volumes of his deceit. "You have an opportunity to become the guardians of the future, gentlemen. If you accept this offer, it will be up to you to decide to whom this gift will be bestowed. Power, gentlemen. Total and absolute power is at your fingertips. If you decide who gets to remember their past, you alone will rule the world."

MALIA COULD scarcely draw breath. But her reaction wasn't one of surprise. She was so furious she saw red.

"That's your offer? The one we can't refuse?" she asked Nicholas, though the question was definitely a rhetorical one. "To give us a glimpse of this magical key so that we can choose among the survivors of the Cataclysm who gets to remember and who doesn't?" Malia turned to face Nicholas, who was still smiling. "That's insane. That's cruel and unjust."

Behind her back, Malia heard Shay say loudly, "That's a horrible thing to say. Do you think we'd be so heinous and greedy as to choose power over the good of our people? We don't care about your offer. We're seeking a remedy to our affliction, not a way to assert power and control over innocent people who just want their old lives back. What you're proposing is monstrous. We'll never agree to such a horrid proposal. Never." By the time Shay ended his rant he was obviously so filled with righteous indignation that he actually trembled with the force of it. Malia was glad to see it.

Dev actually grinned then and cocked a thumb at Shay. "What he said."

Malia had never been more proud to call these men her friends and comrades.

Doctor Lethe seemed unfazed by Shay's outburst. He glanced directly at the doorway behind which Malia and Nicholas stood, unseen because of the gray vapor. Malia whisked around in time to see Nicholas nod firmly.

"What did you do?" Malia asked, clenching her fists in fury.

Nicholas didn't look at her. "We have no use for those who do not cooperate, Malia. If you wish to speak to your friends one last time, I will grant you that chance soon."

About to speak her mind plainly, and possibly jab the tip of her dagger into Nicholas's heartless chest, Malia heard noises of a scuffle in the other room. A group of weird-looking, fishlike men had appeared and captured Dev and Shay. They proceeded to restrain her friends' arms and feet and then disarmed them with ease. Shouting, both Dev and Shay tried to fight back. Stork didn't, but they bound him too. Then the fish men led them from the room.

Malia wasn't a fool. She could act now and kill the leader who stood behind her. But there might well be an army unseen in the shadows—hidden, humanlike but not human, creatures prowling as quiet as the night, waiting to do Nicholas's bidding.

"They won't obey you," Malia said. "And neither will I. None of us will do your bidding. Not ever."

Nicholas chuckled, the vibration low and intimidating. "Wait and see how wrong you are."

THEY DIDN'T have long to wait, which was good since Malia wasn't sure how long she would have been able to bide her time while her companions remained in dire straits. Her worry over Shay's and Dev's fate grew with each breath she took.

Three of those part-human, part-fish creatures returned alongside Doctor Lethe—*and Stork*!

Malia let out a chilly chuckle. "That's how you're gonna beat us? Divide and conquer, eh?" Nicholas merely laughed back in response, as though he hadn't a care in the world.

They stopped in the center of the room, as if staging a theatrical display for Malia's benefit. She was certain that's what it was too, a despicable show delivered in her honor. Doctor Lethe presented the glowing key, lying on his palm like a sacrificial offering, to Stork, who stared at it with greedy, unrelenting eyes.

"Your companions have proven... unsuitable," Doctor Lethe said in his scratchy, thin voice, like rising smoke fumes. "What have you to offer us?"

Malia held her breath, praying Stork remained strong. Where a group prevailed, an individual might feel the temptation and yield. *Stork, in the name of all that's holy, don't do it, don't succumb.*

"I represent a group that can give you whatever you ask for," Stork answered, shocking Malia to the core. What the hell was he talking about?

Doctor Lethe raised an eyebrow, or what would have been an eyebrow except that there was no hair there. "Go on."

"We call ourselves the Sovereign Society," Stork said, pride exuding from his voice. "My people used to rule the world, before the Cataclysm. We want our rightful power back." Stork spoke in simplistic, uncouth phrases, but his meaning came through loud and clear.

"What people are those?" Doctor Lethe asked, his tone betraying nothing.

Stork growled. "The older generation. Senior citizens. The young rule now. But it wasn't always so. We seniors had power over them by law, wealth, and custom. It is only right for us to have that power returned to us."

Malia fisted her hands so tight her nails drew blood from her palms. Her fury knew no bounds.

So Stork—plus an unknown number of other senior citizens—had learned they'd ruled the pre-Cataclysmic world. What had been the source of their dominance? Wealth, connections, control of the seats of power? Malia had seen pictures in books of groups of older men and women said to be in charge of businesses, cities, and even countries. But the Cataclysm had hit the older survivors the hardest because they could not relearn as easily as the young. Clearly they had learned enough to know what they had lost, and they were not happy about having had to yield control to their erstwhile children, who now knew more and adapted better than them.

Of course, Malia mused. This explained why an old man or woman had gotten themselves assigned to every expedition since the start of the Scout and Ranger Corps. Simply so they could find a means to regain their past glory and retake control of the world—by any means necessary, up to and including betraying the young who had tended to them, cared for and respected them, never asking for anything in return.

Petty greed and a loathsome lust for power.

Malia wasn't surprised at yet another display of how low humanity could sink. But she had hoped her traveling companions were better than that. It seemed Stork had failed them all in that regard. She had to give him credit for how thoroughly he'd fooled them, though it made her angry to do so.

"What will you offer us?" Doctor Lethe asked, deadpan.

Stork didn't hesitate. "Whatever you want. As long as we seniors regain *and* retain our positions of power."

Doctor Lethe grinned. The gesture was anything but joyous. Malia was ready, willing, but not able to wipe that smile from his face with her sword. Soon, she vowed to herself. Soon she would show all these abominations what power over life and death waited at the tip of her blade.

"We are in need of people." Doctor Lethe's eyes bore into Stork, who seemed unfazed by the demand. "That is all. No power, no gold, no means of transportation, absolutely no resources of any kind. Will you give us people?"

Stork nodded firmly. "Yes. We have many young ones we can send to you as soon as you wish."

As Malia imagined ripping out his throat and his tongue, silencing him then and there, Stork dropped his gaze to the glowing key. "Will you give me my memory back?"

Doctor Lethe bowed his head slightly. "Of course. That was to be our first offer. As a sign of good faith between us and as a pledge of our mutual agreement. Please, touch the key and close your eyes. Your memory, in its entirety, will be restored. This I vow."

Stork closed his eyes, a satisfied smile dancing on his lips, and with determination pressed his palm against the radiant artifact.

A bright white light blinded Malia, but only for an instant.

Then she saw… it.

A GLOWING white… *thing* with tiny delicate tendrils somehow emerged from inside the key, slowly pulling itself forward until it was out all the way. Stork didn't seem to be aware of its presence. Once the pulsating, globular wet mass of something rubbery but alive was free, it sped up, using its tentacles to climb Stork's arm as fast as a spider. The blissful expression on Stork's face never changed.

"Stork, stop!" Malia slammed her fists on the energy field keeping her from the room, but to no effect. "Open your eyes!"

The little squid creature veered around Stork's neck, leaving a trail of goo in its wake. Latching on to his nape, the creature made a suctioning sound. It attached itself to the base of Stork's skull, at the top of his spinal column. Its glow dimmed, and the thing seemed to meld directly into Stork's body, until it could be seen no more.

Malia trembled with disgust, well aware that it was far too late to intervene—at least for Stork. Perhaps there was still time to save Shay and Dev.

Stork opened his eyes. The blissful look had vanished. In its place was a dull, vacant expression—empty eyes, slightly agape mouth, and all traces of intellect and will gone.

In essence, Stork now resembled all the other less-than-human denizens of Innsmouth, save for Nicholas and Doctor Lethe. *A mindless slave.* One of those slimy, slithery creatures that shied away from light, barely spoke, and shuffled about feeble-mindedly, mere drones. They bore only a vague likeness to human beings, but in the end humanity seemed like a mere afterthought in their creation or transformation. The horrid notion that they might have once been real humans awakened no pity in Malia. Stork still retained his human appearance, though, so Malia assumed the fishy effect on his looks took a certain amount of time to form.

"Is anything left of him within?" Malia asked, whispering through clenched teeth.

"Not anything you would recognize," Nicholas replied coolly. "But we didn't lie. His memories are now restored. He knows who he is. A slave to our will." Nicholas spoke low into her ear. "Humans are sheep. They were created to obey without question, to follow the shepherd."

"You?" Malia spat out vehemently through gritted teeth. "Will you do this to me and to my other friends too? Like the ones living here?"

"Stork has a mission to fulfill first." Nicholas's voice oozed pride and malice. "See for yourself."

Doctor Lethe addressed Stork with a satisfied smile. "Who are you?"

No affect appeared on Stork's face as he replied, "Andrew Warren. I'm an investment banker on Wall Street." His voice was toneless, as though he were merely reciting indifferent information from memory with no personal connection to what he said.

Doctor Lethe grinned wider. "Whom do you serve?"

Stork stayed impassive. "Father Dagon and Mother Hydra."

Malia frowned. Those names meant nothing to her. Yet she instinctively feared them.

"What is your mission?" Doctor Lethe asked.

Stork looked like he was dreaming awake, or perhaps sleepwalking. "I will return to Canal City through the portal and ensure that everyone in the Sovereign Society will come here to Innsmouth with able-bodied crews you can transform into your willing servants or offer on your bloodied altars as tribute. All shall bow before the deep glory of Father Dagon and Mother Hydra."

"Good." Doctor Lethe smirked, seeming pleased. "We will give you machines that will ensure your group's speedy arrival back to us." He waved a hand about. Two fish men came and escorted Stork from the room. Stork didn't resist.

Malia accepted then and there that the Stork she knew was gone. "What was that thing that attached itself to him?"

"An Echenecus," Nicholas explained dryly. "A conduit. Part of a larger entity. Impossible to remove through surgical or chemical means." Nicholas took hold of her arm, his grip tightening with every breath she drew. "And now, it's your turn."

"*No!*"

Like shadows springing to life, residents of Innsmouth appeared out of thin air to take charge of her. Malia struggled in vain, fighting back with all her might. She employed every combat technique she knew, delivering fierce kicks and sharp blows to those around her.

As delighted as she was that it took eight of the fish men to carry her through the wall of energy, Malia predicted defeat. She was vastly outnumbered. And these fish men seemed to possess physical strength beyond that of a normal man. But that didn't mean she was about to surrender. *No way in hell!*

Doctor Lethe shoved the shimmering artifact in front of her.

Malia squirmed, her mind's eye envisioning one of those squid things wrapping around her body and mind with its slimy tentacles, and she cried out in useless fury.

Three of the gray-skinned goons forced her down on her knees, grabbed her hand, and unceremoniously slapped it on top of the key.

A blinding shard of awareness pierced the dark veil of her consciousness.

Where there'd been the blackness of ignorance now shone the light of knowledge. Swirls of alien color swam around her, blurring her vision.

The pain was gone in an instant.

But no squid-like creature had touched her body, mind, or soul.

Malia opened her eyes slowly. The room spun and twisted around her at odd angles of rippling madness. The utter otherworldliness of it all emanated from within her, projected onto all she witnessed. A familiarity arose from her core.

Nothing *alien* had touched her body, mind, or soul. The epiphany rattled her brain.

She stood up on shaky legs, growing steadier by the second. Her sentience reeled and regrouped as she made her way back to the life she had lost in the Cataclysm.

With an inner calm she'd longed for, Malia faced Nicholas, whom she now knew—and had always known—as Nyarlathotep.

He smiled enigmatically. "Welcome home… *sister*."

CHAPTER 7

"OH DEV, what are we going to do now?" Shay's voice quivered. He heard it distinctly in his own ears, a desperate wail and plea. He glanced at Dev, knowing what to expect. Grimacing, Dev undoubtedly hated hearing the smallness, the fear, the uncertainty in Shay's tone. They were trapped, but as far as Dev was concerned they had hope still. Shay knew this about Dev well. It was what made Dev a great leader and an honorable, strong man.

"We're gonna escape, we're gonna find our friends, and we're gonna fly away from this terrible place." Dev's voice rumbled deep in his chest. Shay wanted nothing more than to believe him. Shay had to have faith; he had to because he was on the verge of collapsing from the mental strain. Only Dev's determination lent him fortitude.

The old cell in which they'd been imprisoned reeked of something alive but rotting. Smelly hay covered the floor, and a rusty, ancient army-style cot topped with a bare, dirty mattress was the only furniture. The air was chilly and damp enough to induce coughing fits. The walls, floor, and ceiling were concrete, with slivers picked or scratched away here and there by tiny sharp implements—or by fingernails. Clearly they weren't the first or the only occupants to share these unpleasant accommodations.

But they were alone. Those who had brought them here and locked them inside had vanished hours ago. There were no guards; just a lock for which they had no key. Therefore they had no hope of escape on their own. Lockpicking wasn't a skill rangers or scouts were required to learn. If they ever got back home, Shay would change that policy.

Shay hugged himself to ward off the cold, but icy claws had already taken hold of his insides.

Dev closed the gap between them, his gait firm, his gaze steady. He gripped Shay's arms with his big hands, stopping Shay's trembling. Shay closed his eyes and let his anxiety fall away at the touch of his powerful man.

Except… Dev wasn't Shay's man. Unfortunately.

Tears stung his eyes. He needed to be touched. Really touched and held and loved. He needed Dev.

As though sensing his underlying need, Dev slid his hands up to cup Shay's face, his fingers tender. "I won't let anything bad happen to you, Shay. I swear it. Over my dead body."

Shay let out a watery gasp. "Don't say that. I couldn't bear it if you…." Even finishing the thought out loud was impossible, like it was a damn spell, conjuring misfortune and misery upon them.

Dev brought Shay firmly against his chest in a tight embrace. He even rocked a little. Shay was certain this was what a perfect world was like. "I'm not going anywhere, Shay. I'm going nowhere without you." Dev drew in a sharp breath, as though he had more to say, but then he snapped his mouth shut, growing silent.

Praying for Dev to finish what he'd intended to say, Shay waited, breathless with desire and craving that elusive, tentative heart-to-heart connection Dev sometimes alluded to.

But the door to the cellblock opened, rusty hinges creaking sharply. Malia walked toward them, her expression wary, her movements cautious. She dropped a black duffel bag on the ground, a loud thump echoing off the stone walls. Then she rested her hands on the bars and offered a small smile. "Hi, guys. You okay?"

Shay rushed to her, trying to hug her through the bars, as awkward as that was. Breathless, he asked, "What happened to you? Are you okay? Did they hurt you?"

Malia shushed him, patting his hand gently. "Calm down, Shay, before you give yourself a coronary." She frowned, stopped midsentence, and let out a baffled chuckle. "What a funny word. I don't think I've ever used it before."

Dev approached them, guarded, coming to stand at Shay's side. "What happened? Are you hurt?" Shay was proud of him, how cool and composed he sounded, and yet concerned for their companion— even if he had feelings for her boyfriend. Or so Shay dared to hope.

Malia hesitated, her frown remaining. "I suppose that's a matter of interpretation." She blinked several times and then refocused on Shay and Dev, managing a tight smile. "Listen. We don't have much time."

"What's going on?" Shay asked, exactly at the same moment as Dev said, "Report."

Malia's expression grew so furious and vengeful Shay almost stepped back in fear of being the target of all that emotion. "Stork's betrayed us."

"*What*?" Shay and Dev asked in unison.

Malia nodded grimly. "Apparently Stork belongs to a secret group of older people who want their former stations of power back—by any means necessary. Stork has touched the key and regained his memories. But… he's their slave now, a mindless drone. There's a… a creature attached to his brain and spine, controlling him."

Dev cocked his head as if contemplating the sheer madness of her words. "A creature…?"

Malia nodded, vexation and worry warring in her expression. "Yes. A small squid-like thing with tentacles it used to latch on to Stork. Then it… sort of phased out of sight, becoming invisible." She shook her head as if trying to refocus on the matter at hand. "In short, Stork's no longer with us. He made a deal with these Innsmouth people to retake the world for the elderly, with all the young in the world to be the payment. It was a fool's bargain, for he and his fellows will be enslaved as well. The physiological change in them will be slow and subtle at first, but in the end they will become exactly like the Innsmouth folk, their memories intact but their personalities and will obliterated. The contract is thus fulfilled to the letter but not in accordance with its spirit. Nonetheless, Stork will keep his end of the deal. He has no choice, not with that creature stuck inside his head calling the shots. He will convince the other elders who are in league with him to come to this town, and they will betray and hand over the young to become slaves in turn. Slaves and—" She swallowed, looking sickly and disgusted as she shoved the words out past her lips. "—other things. You two have to escape, get back to the ship, and fly out of here as fast as you can. You understand?"

Dev appeared ready to contest the issue but finally nodded, as rigid and unrelenting as Malia.

But Shay wasn't ready to accept what Malia was hinting at. "You're coming with us, aren't you, Malia?"

Her gaze landed on him. Everything was there, the gloomy determination, the refusal, the underlying strength of conviction. "No, Shay. I'm not coming with you."

"Malia…." Shay squeezed her hands, desperate, tears in his eyes, his heart pounding its way out of his chest, a terrible dread hollowing him out. "I'm *not* leaving without you."

She smiled back then, a radiant, happy gesture. Immediately the room felt lighter and brighter and the situation less dismal and deadly. "Of all the people I've known in my long life, you, Shay, are the very best. The absolute best. You've given me kindness, friendship, love, pleasure, and a life the meaning of which I never understood before you."

Shay shook his head adamantly, so angry at the hopeless change of events he wanted to shout and hit something. "No, don't say that. That sounds like good-bye, and I… I can't let this be the end. Please, Malia, come with us. If you love me—"

"That's funny. My name *is* Malia." She chuckled for a second or two, but then the sound died in her throat. Her big hazel eyes grew serious and pleaded with Shay, who refused to even entertain the notion of leaving her behind. "I can't come with you, dearest. I wish I could. You have no idea how badly I wish I could."

"Why can't you?" Shay begged. Not even one of Dev's gentle hands on his shoulder helped. "Please, Malia. I can't live without you." It was true—from a certain point of view. Though the quality of his love for her had changed, that took nothing away from the grandeur and impact of it. To him, she was irreplaceable.

Malia chuckled, touching the tip of his nose with the tip of her finger. "Silly boy. You are in my heart. Forever." Before Shay had a chance to argue his intent to keep her close, Malia took Shay's hand and placed it on top of Dev's hand where it rested on a bar. "Shay, love. Be who you are and always were meant to be. Be true to your heart. Love is too important to waste on indecision or fear. The world has forgotten hate. It's buried in the past, as it should be. So, love, dare to dream and risk your heart. Dev here is well worth it."

At Shay's side, Dev went rigid. His voice trembled as he said, "Malia, I would never have done anything behind your back."

"Believe me, Dev, I know." Her smile at the both of them was kind, understanding, and final. "Shay, I should have set you free to follow your heart long ago. Forgive me for being so selfish. Your company warmed my heart and eased my soul every single day."

Shay sobbed. He had loved Malia for many winters. In a way he still did and always would. But his fingers entwined with Dev's, purely on instinct.

So Malia had known of their hidden emotions for a while. She wasn't aghast at the idea and didn't want to stand between Shay and Dev. She released Shay of all obligations to her. Thanks to her, he was free—at least he would be if all went according to plan.

Shay had never felt so conflicted, torn between needing Malia near as a beloved friend, and needing to be with Dev in every sense of the word. Dev pulled Shay into his arms and held him through the sorrow and pain. "Why, Malia?" Shay kept asking into Dev's chest.

Malia's voice cracked but only once. It simply strengthened as she went on. "I can't come with you. There're far too many dangerous collusions happening. Upon his return, Stork is bringing an armada of skyships here so that the old can regain their memories and the young can be enslaved to seal the deal."

Dev stiffened, his tone harsh and demanding. "How soon?"

"Nic—um, Stork was shown an instant means of travel through a portal. It'd take too long to explain it. Suffice it to say, the skyships will be arriving here in no time. And once they do… everything we've worked for will be for naught, everyone we know will be destroyed, and our common future will be a thing of the past. Once you leave on the *Smoke Sparrow*, I hope that you'll be able to intercept the fleet before it reaches Innsmouth and that you can convince the young crewmembers of a real danger to their persons if they blindly continue to follow orders."

"How did you learn all this?" Dev asked, his voice tense and suspicious enough for Shay to move out of his embrace and study both speakers with a sense of foreboding.

Malia's jaw quivered as her eyes flashed like steel. "I too was forced to touch the Key. I remember who I was before the Cataclysm."

Shay gasped in horror, imagining a tiny squid embedded into her skull. "No...."

Dev growled. "Does that make you their slave as well?"

Malia closed her eyes, squeezing them tight, a deep and profound sorrow twisting her beauty briefly. "No, I'm... I'm different. I'm not a slave. I'm a...." Her eyes opened. A bleak light of hopelessness was there and gone. A deep-seated hatred filled her words and her tone turned dark and deadly. "I'm a master. I'm... one of them."

SHAY STARED, disbelieving. "That's... impossible. No! That can't be true!"

Dev clearly had his scruples since his tone remained level as he said, "Shay's right. The Cataclysm happened over twenty winters ago. You'd have been an infant."

"No." Malia exhaled deeply. "I never knew how to tell you. But when I awoke... I was as you see me now. All grown up. I haven't changed at all since that day."

The confession hit her hard, Shay could tell. "Why didn't you tell us? Why didn't you tell... me?" His heart was breaking, cracks now, full-blown shards soon, and ashes by the time this day would be done and buried.

Malia looked down, camouflaging her shame, a state of mind Shay could understand. "No one else I met was like me. I didn't understand why, so I waited and watched. Winters passed, and still there were none like me in Canal City." Her chin lifted as her anger came off her in waves. "Now I know why."

Dev inched Shay behind his back, the act slow but steady. "You're one of our captors? The odd fish-looking folk?"

Malia shook her head and frowned. "No, not like them. I'm something… else, something different. I'm a… a higher form of life. If the people of Innsmouth were frogs, I would be a frog goddess. I am superior to them. I cannot be enslaved. I will not become like them, perhaps ever. In that aspect, I think, I resemble more those beings Nic—their leader talked about. Cosmic creatures likened unto gods, eternal entities that never change."

"But what do they want with us? What do *you* want with us?" Dev didn't sound hurt or betrayed but as a man trying to make sense of new information.

Shay elbowed his way back to Dev's side. "Don't talk to her like that. She said she's *not* one of them. She never will be. She's our friend and our companion. She'd never hurt us." Shay believed in her. No matter what. He couldn't fathom the mentality of a person who could harm someone they'd loved. For Shay, the act was inconceivable and unconscionable. "Malia, I don't care that you're from here. You're not with these people who mean to hurt us. I still care for you. You're not like them. I'll always believe and have faith in you."

Malia's eyes glistened. Her smile was soft and mournful. "That's why you're the best person I've ever known. I love you very much. You'll ever be my best friend." Her gaze flicked to Dev. "But we have bigger problems at the moment. When I touched the silver key and remembered again, I learned what caused the Cataclysm."

As Malia explained what she knew of times past, Shay almost didn't believe her. He didn't want to. He didn't even understand everything she said. A part of him, a suspicious corner of his mind, was certain Malia was withholding something essential. She had a secret. But… perhaps she kept it to spare them further horrible revelations and the insanity sure to follow.

One thing came through loud and clear, though: the human race had played a key role in enabling the Cataclysm to befall. Among the wonderful inventions and machines humans had built were terrible devices created for a single purpose: mass destruction. They had been released by humans on their fellow man in wars for territory, struggles for resources, or with the intent of wiping out opposing ideologies with murder and mayhem. The end result was surely not what anyone had intended or envisioned, but be that as it may, Shay found the idea that humanity had done this to itself virtually unthinkable. And yet, here they were, stuck in the middle of an unavoidable truth and trapped in an indisputable reality.

Dev, as usual, seemed to be on top of more practical things. "Escaping this town will be difficult."

Malia grinned, nearly back to her own self, the woman Shay loved and admired. "Yes, but you're a captain and a leader. You thrive on challenges. I'll ensure a safe getaway from this cell. Beyond that, you're on your own. Take this." Through the bars Malia handed Dev a folded piece of paper.

Dev turned it around in his hand. "What is it?"

"It's a sketch of the underbelly of this town I drew in haste. What you need to focus on are those underground passages. They run through town, often connecting with the sewers. They're your best bet for moving unseen back to the lighthouse and the ship. This, combined with Shay's maps of Innsmouth, should be extremely helpful."

"Thanks. This'll come in handy," Dev said, unrolling the map and studying it quickly with discerning eyes before folding it up again and stashing it under his jacket.

Malia pointed behind her at the black bag. "Your weapons and equipment are in there. They should aid you." She fumbled inside her corset pocket, just tiny enough to hide a lockpick or a key. She fished out a rusty iron key and extended it to Dev through the bars. "That's the key to the cell. Once I'm gone, use it. And once you reach the ship, fly away as fast as you can."

"What about you?" Thank goodness Dev asked the question. Shay wasn't sure he could let out a single utterance without a barrage of tears blinding him. His heart hurt. There was nothing he could do about it.

"I'll do what I can to make sure you get away safe and sound." Her steely gaze kept a tight lock on Dev as she said, "One way or another, this town and everyone in it must be destroyed. As of right now, all other goals become irrelevant. This place must fall." She gripped Dev's hand on the bar, her hold white-knuckled. "Do you understand?"

Dev nodded, equally determined and resolute. The inner strength they demonstrated impressed—and frightened—Shay, who only hoped he could rise to the occasion and do what had to be done in order to be seen as worthy in the eyes of those he loved and admired.

"If you see anyone down there in the passages, or if they see you," Malia said firmly, "leave none alive. Not a single one of those creatures can be allowed to escape. Even if… if they belong to familiar faces you've known for ages. They mean to transform everyone from Canal City and the airships. Save those you can, but kill the rest."

Shay implored, "But how can we? How are we to tell the difference between friend and foe?"

"These beings might once have been humans, but they lack the ability to express affect. They show no emotion on their faces. They'll be blank and void of all feelings you can think of. They can mimic voices, with traces of sentiment and humanity, but they are false. They do, however, understand and utilize human motivations, like pain and fear, greed and need, obsession and addiction. That is their persuasion, their arsenal of seduction. Many will undoubtedly succumb. Save those who won't; abandon the rest."

Shay shook his head, practically frantic. "They're our friends and—"

"I am cruel to be kind," Malia cut him off, her tone gravelly and somber. "What you loved about our friends will no longer be there. Those you see will be nothing more than husks, shells for those creatures to use to get close to you and kill you. Do not be fooled by their false faces and persuasive words. They are not human anymore. Another thing… do *not* let them get close to you. They're mindless drones now, without personalities, but they're wicked fast and strong as steel."

"We'll be careful," Dev said firmly.

"Good." Malia sounded relieved. Then her voice tensed again. "I can offer this piece of advice. Those small squids attached to humans are part of a larger entity; kill one, all are alerted. Also, they come from the deep-ocean trenches, so they need human hosts to see in the light."

Dev snapped his fingers as a light bulb went off in his head. "So that's why there were no fires or lanterns lit in the lodge."

"One of the main reasons, yes," Malia confirmed. "Use your portable gas lanterns if need be. They can be covered for covert actions and lit up brightly in case they charge at you." She gripped the bars tight, her knuckles white as snow. "And whatever happens, do *not* touch that silver key. If you do, one of those things will attach itself to you, and the real you will be lost forever."

"We understand." Dev sounded cold and callous. Shay was about to rip him to shreds. But then Dev glanced at Shay under his brow. His face betrayed everything he felt—which mirrored everything Shay felt too. Like him, Dev was losing a friend and companion. And just like Shay, Dev hated the idea.

But they had no choice. Malia had made a decision. She had that right. Shay and Dev had to accept that, no matter how deeply it tore them up inside. They'd deal with the fallout later, if and when there was a later to be had.

Dev regarded Malia, his brows scrunched together. "What's your plan?"

Malia quirked an eyebrow, a headstrong gesture. "I will burn this place to ashes." She pointed a finger at the both of them. "You two had better not be here when I do."

BEYOND LAST minute advice, they had no more to share, so they all stood in awkward silence. There was much to say, but no real chance to speak one's mind without adding to the hurt and anguish already hanging heavy above them. Anything more would drag the situation on, with no hope of resolution or ease. But Shay had to ask himself: Was separation ever supposed to be effortless if and when emotions were involved? Malia had been so important to him for so long, he didn't know how to be without her.

Not to mention the likelihood she was walking headfirst into her own death.

No more Malia. The dreadful thought filled Shay with soul-crunching pain.

Shay gulped, his lips numb with all the worrying he'd done trying to prevent pleading words from escaping them. Even if they weren't destined to be together, Shay didn't want Malia to die. She'd given her understanding, empathetic consent to Shay and Dev pursuing the attraction that simmered just beneath the surface. That alone demonstrated the depth of her honorable character. For her to be gone forever, it would be a loss, diminishing humanity's chances of survival and growing out of their infancy.

With all that in mind, Shay whispered, "Malia? If you can, don't throw yourself into death needlessly. Come find us again and join us in Canal City. We'll welcome you with open arms, no matter what. You're family."

Dev's deep voice rumbled at his side. "I agree with Shay, Malia. It has been an honor to stand at your side and call you friend. I hope I get the opportunity to do so again in the future." At that moment, Shay couldn't have loved him more.

Malia stared back at them, eyes wide, their brown depths misty. Her jaw quivered and a flicker of a smile emerged to brighten their dark situation. "I… I'll try. I promise." She glanced at the door to the cellblock, as though she sensed the arrival of one of these monstrosities. "Now go. Don't waste any more time. Go."

A blink of an eye later she was gone, practically vanished into thin air.

As if he were mortally wounded, Shay clutched at his chest, unable to breathe with the compression of sorrow within and without his heart. Hot tears ran down his cheeks, for a part of him predicted he'd never see Malia again.

Dev wound his arms around Shay and buried him against his chest, swaying slightly. "We'll see her again," he said in his deep rumbling voice, as though he were telepathically linked to Shay. "Don't lose hope. Have faith in her and in us."

Shay nodded frantically, his body pressed to the solid warmth of his Dev, and took a leap of faith. "Yes." Sniffling and wiping his runny nose on his sleeve, Shay pushed himself out of the embrace, as hard as it was. "She's bought us some time. Let's make the best of it, shall we?"

Dev nodded with a brave, encouraging smile. "Let's get out of here."

He shoved the old key into the cell door lock, twisted and jiggled it until the lock clicked, and pushed the door open with a rusty creak. Both men cringed. All they could do was continue on with the escape and hope these Innsmouth people believed they were so much smarter than humans, the prisoners wouldn't even conceive of the notion of escape.

Dev grabbed the black bag, opened it, and pulled out their weapons and equipment.

"All of it?" Shay asked, already arming himself, just in case.

"Yup." Dev's gruff response was so like him that despite their dire circumstances and even worse odds of survival, Shay grinned. If they did live to tell the tale, he would enjoy his future life with Dev to the fullest. "How much ammo have you got?"

Shay checked his inventory fast, as he was well used to such preparations for the worst-case scenario. "Six collision grenades, twelve cartridges for the stunshine gun, and of course, the shock stick. You?"

"The same. Basic armament only." Frowning, Dev looked worried, although to Shay his expression when he focused his resolve was much the same. "We have to use our weapons sparingly. We don't know how many hostiles we're going to encounter, so we can't go in guns blazing."

Shay snorted. "I wasn't under the impression we would." He grew serious and solemn. "I'll be careful. You do the same."

Dev nodded back, a small, lopsided grin showcasing his pride in Shay.

As soon as they abandoned their former cell, Dev turned toward the door that led to the stairs and the ground floor.

Shay grasped at his jacket sleeve. "Where are you going? Malia's map takes us down a level, not up."

Dev grinned. "Yeah, I know. I'm gonna break the lock on the back door and leave it ajar so our pursuers, if there are any, will think we fled to the streets, not below ground."

Shay raised his eyebrows, impressed as usual. "Smart thinking. I'll wait here."

Dev skulked out the door and up the stairs, disappearing into the shadows. He wasn't gone for more than a minute or two before he came back and gave a thumbs-up. Shay rolled his eyes, but mirth bloomed in his heart and endowed him with a healthy dose of courage.

The second underground level of the dungeon smelled of chilled air and rat droppings. None of the cells were occupied, so they snuck past them with ease. A drain on the floor sluiced icy, dirty waters down to the sewers. Next to it was a manhole. Swampy moss and filthy gravel covered it, proving no one had used that route in ages.

Dev swept the garbage aside, gripped the slimy handle, and slowly yanked the heavy manhole cover open. An unholy racket of screeching metal followed. Dev and Shay both heaved a sigh. It would have been a miracle if nothing had gone wrong.

Deciding that waiting for company to arrive to restrain or kill them was foolish, Dev waved Shay closer. Stale, moldy air puffed upward, and Shay reared back. After Dev glared at him, Shay coughed to clear his throat and his embarrassment. He gripped the slick metal ladder with both hands and began his cautious descent.

Strangely, no sounds of any kind emerged from above or below.

Still, Shay wasn't naïve enough to believe their escape would go unnoticed for long.

Rank, putrid odors wafted up to greet him as he made his way down. The metal rungs felt cold and clammy against his skin, and he had to grip them hard to avoid slipping to his death. Peering below provided no clues. Only a dark vapor was visible. Above him, Shay felt the tremors on the ladder as Dev followed. A muffled metal clank told him Dev had closed the lid.

Shay's leg thudded jarringly as he met with the bottom instead of another rung.

Wincing, he called out in a stage whisper, "Hit rock bottom. So to speak."

Shay wiped his hands on his pants while he turned around, trying to make out anything in the dark gloom. He definitely stood on rough solid stones, so there had to be ledges around the actual sewer. A low gush indicated water did run through the channel. A few louder drips here and there suggested the existence of pools of calmer waters.

A small thump signaled Dev's arrival in the sewers. "You okay?" he asked.

Shay nodded, then realized Dev couldn't see the gesture. "Yes."

Dev fished a compass and Malia's sketchy map out of his pocket, and Shay lit the gas lantern. It was a delicate piece of artistic functionality, able to fit on a palm, with shutters that could control how much light it emitted.

Dev pointed at the compass and the map. "According to the map, the jail is a block or two from the Marsh memorial Malia and I passed on our way into town. We're close to the harbor. If we follow the compass east, we'll be back onboard *Smoke Sparrow* in no time."

"Lead on, oh fearless leader." Shay smirked at Dev's fierce stare.

Shay kept the slightly overlapping shutters close to their minimum setting, so only tiny rays of light illuminated the sewers. Curtains of moss hung from the arched ceiling above. Murky waters flowed lazily in the dark channel, the sound less restful than it might have been under different circumstances. The passageway was large enough to fit narrow walkways on both sides of the canal and thus allowed for Shay and Dev to progress almost side by side, with Shay holding the lantern and Dev gripping his stunshine rifle.

After a couple of twists and turns, they heard the sloshing patter of feet ahead.

Shay turned the lantern off, and Dev cocked his rifle. Crouching down, they waited to see what would come around the bend.

But no one emerged in their line of sight.

Clearly tense, Dev waved for Shay to stay put while he investigated. Shay didn't want to get left behind or for Dev to go on alone, even if for minor reconnaissance. But he was used to this kind of treatment as a scholar, not a combatant, so he gritted his teeth and set out to wait.

Patience had never been easy for Shay, who didn't like sitting on his hands, waiting for something to happen. He wasn't a passive person. Granted, when it came to Dev and other scouts and rangers in positions of leadership, Shay tended to assume the submissive role, the one to follow, obey, and carry out orders rather than issuing them. And yes, he did have the habit of losing himself in the books he studied, forgetting the world, occasionally at the most inopportune moments imaginable.

But no such distractions were available then and there. No one to tell Shay what to do and no literary masterpieces to guide him through gut-wrenchingly challenging situations with their unerring, insightful example.

Thankfully, Shay didn't have long to wait. Dev returned quickly, slinking through the darkness with the agility, swiftness, and silence of a black cat.

"No go," Dev hissed, even his hushed tone tinted with frustration. "The only passage due east is blocked off."

"A barricade?" Shay asked, puzzled at how fast their escape had been noticed.

"No." Dev shook his head. "Looks like a natural cave-in. The ceiling and sections of the wall seem to have collapsed. I could see the sky. There are two of those fish guys there, pacing mostly, clearing the rubble one brick at a time, going slow. They'll be at it for dozens of winters at their current pace. I guess repairs aren't a priority for them."

"What now?" Shay asked. His fears already murmured in his ears what was ahead.

"We have to find a way around them," Dev said, confirming Shay's doubts. "This can't be the only passage leading to the harbor." He rubbed his jaw, his beard creating a scratching sound. "These underground halls explain why I felt like we were being watched the first time we walked along Water Street, hugging the harbor."

"I don't like the idea of having to go deeper into the town to get out of it," Shay said. He felt cowardly saying it, but he had a seriously bad feeling. He couldn't explain it. His instincts cried out for attention, demanding he pay heed to the warnings and not wander deeper into enemy territory. "Especially since Malia pointed out we don't have much time. The skyships will be here soon, and whatever she plans will undoubtedly leave nothing but a smoldering crater where this town used to be."

Dev brushed his fingertips across Shay's cheek, giving him shivers of cold and flashes of heat at once. "I will get both of us out of here. I promise. Trust me."

As Shay locked gazes with Dev's beautiful eyes, gray as the winter seas, he decided to take a leap of faith, one of many he'd undertaken during this voyage. His doubts were a thing of the past with the man he loved standing at his side.

"I'll trust you till my dying breath, Dev."

Chapter 8

THE BRIGHT light and unwavering faith in Shay's sky-blue eyes spoke of hope and love in a resplendent way words failed to describe. Dev was a goner. And he beamed at the loyalty and confidence his beloved showered him with.

He spoke gruffly, his cheeks flushing with heat. "Thanks, Shay. Let's get this show on the road."

With cautious glimpses over their shoulders, they snuck back the way they came until they had retraced their steps to a junction that separated into three paths. The eastern path was out, so their options included only the northwest and southwest directions.

A single glance of mutual agreement spoke volumes, and Dev led Shay on to the southwest passage. Their path was soon encroached upon by walls of water cascading from cracked slivers in the ceiling, revealing that their route took them right underneath the rapids of the Manuxet River. No matter how quickly they jumped past the watery veils, there was no chance for them to avoid getting drenched by chilly autumn gushes.

The water level soon rose to their calves, and the foul stench swamped them. A couple of half-eaten dead fish floated on the muddy sewer sludge. Bits of plants, rubbish, sticks, and mutilated rat bodies streamed past their feet until they had to cover their noses and mouths with cloth to block the vomit-inducing stink. Not even traversing the curved walkway prevented firsthand contact with organic debris, garbage, and waste.

Like Dev wasn't creeped out enough by all the unnatural weirdness around them.

But for Shay's sake, he'd remain strong. Neither of them could afford weakness until they could put this miserable town behind them. There'd be no shedding of tears, no falling and breaking down, no despair or surrender. Malia would do what she had said; of that Dev was certain.

"Can you see which way we're headed?" Shay asked on his heels, sounding anxious. His lantern remained unlit, so they navigated by touch and by the faintly glowing blue moss and green mushrooms that sparkled unexpected colors and shimmers of light into the dim.

"I can see the compass fine." Well, with some squinting, anyway, Dev mused to himself. The various sewer junctions, spreading like the tentacles of deep-ocean monsters, appeared as shady, dark openings, like mouths ready to devour them alive. "I'm following the passageways that keep us close to the coast. Or at least that's what I'm trying to do."

Shay let out a surprised chuckle that lightened the mood like a lit candle in a dark room. "Aha. Well, I'm sure there's nothing you can't handle, my brave captain." His wink, all but salacious, gave Dev a warm flush and heart palpitations.

Even if Shay was using flirtation to push aside his impending loss of Malia.

"Come on, my saucy little minx," Dev said with a hiccup-y chuckle.

Their heartfelt exchange had been a ray of sunlight in the middle of their trek through an unknown underground. But what awaited them in the heart of darkness was more than monsters; there skulked imprisonment, slavery, brainwashing, and loss of those nearest and dearest. Intangible they were, but they meant the world. Dev couldn't believe how easy it was to lose sight of that little fact.

AFTER AN interval filled with nothing but eerie silence, they came across another cave-in, this one showing burned timbers, ash piles, and singed fireman's equipment. The way forward was blocked entirely by the back of a fire truck where it had fallen through the concrete floor. One corner of the metal was twisted and punctured, and what water had been inside the tanker had spilled into the sewers long ago.

Dev checked the map. "We're on the south side of the Manuxet River. Right under the fire station." He frowned when he pinpointed their precise location, angry at himself for not paying enough attention to the path ahead, as unfamiliar as it was. "We're pretty fucking far from the coast. Dammit," he cursed, wrinkling the map in his hands as they fisted in frustration.

Shay rested a warm hand on his arm, squeezing gently. "Don't worry. We'll find our way regardless." At the moment Shay's faith in Dev seemed blind and unfounded. But Dev drew strength and courage from that fountain of love.

He couldn't hold back the impulse any longer.

Stuffing the map and compass into his pockets and his rifle into his back holster, Dev cupped Shay's face, stroked his smooth skin and silky curls with care and tenderness, and brushed his mouth over Shay's delightfully plump lips.

Shay let out a quick shocked gasp. The act parted his mouth. Dev used this window of opportunity to glide his tongue in deeper, to explore Shay's taste to the fullest.

No longer caught unawares, Shay wrapped his arms around Dev's broad shoulders, his grip on Dev's coat and exposed neck tight, and rose up on tiptoe to get closer. With wordless permission given, Dev wound his own arms about Shay's waist and upper back. He pulled Shay flush against himself. Shay's young and nimble form bent with a full-body tremble. An insatiable hunger filled Dev. Heat arced between them, bordering on unbearable need.

Moving forward blindly, Dev ravaged Shay's mouth and simultaneously shoved Shay up against the sewer wall, pinning the slender man with his bulkier size, heavier weight, and greater height. Dev needed the leverage to do as he pleased. And, *oh boy*, did he have a lot planned for just this contingency. He'd begin with inhaling Shay's scent, his hair and skin. He'd let his hands roam freely, sneaking them underneath Shay's clothes to feel his smooth, heated skin, and then he'd use his mouth to follow that same path down to—

A loud splash close by startled both men. Wildly, they peered in all directions, trying to see what was unseen. With experience and caution, Dev made sure they were concealed by most of the rubble from the collapsed ceiling. Plus, the fire engine kept them in the shadows. But movement could draw attention easier than being seen in the light, even in near-total darkness, so both men froze and held their breath.

A sparkle of light underwater in the channel heralded the splashing burst as a single man jumped up from the water like a flying fish. He must have dove under the fire truck, using the canal flow to swim under the blockage.

Unlike a flying fish, though, the Innsmouthian man broke the swirling surface with a leap, landing on his feet with bent knees. Dripping, he rambled sluggishly toward the passage Dev and Shay had come from. He didn't notice or care about the two onlookers, both fraught with fear and worry that any second he would look back and see them.

But the creature did nothing of the sort, instead slowly making his way to the shadows. He didn't even appear to be searching for anyone. Perhaps he was just… taking a stroll, Dev mused, in the… sewers….

Shay said nothing. Dev sensed how scared he was, but he was still handling it, somehow. Shay pointed at the fish man lumbering away without a care in the world. Dev knew what had caught his companion's eye.

As the barely human creature vanished into the dark, the squid glimmered, fully visible. Like other deep-sea organisms, the thing lit up in vibrant, rich, bioluminescent colors, ranging from electric blue, forest green, and royal purple to fiery orange, bloodred, and golden yellow. The colors shimmered with a detectable rhythmic beat, probably its regular pulse. Its tentacles latched on to the man's body—all over, in fact, visible even beneath his clothes.

The fish man himself was lost from sight in the darkness, but the squid attached to him remained discernible until it—they— disappeared beyond the curvature of the sewers.

Dev felt Shay's rapid heartbeat and the exact moment when he released his held breath in a gush of air. "Oh. Oh. Is that what you saw? Before, in the tunnel?"

"I saw a glimpse of colorful lights, but I didn't see what created it this clearly. It must have been those squid things Malia mentioned."

Trying not to shudder but failing, Dev gathered his strength of will and courage and regained his position of command. "We'd better move on. I don't want to be here in case that thing decides to double back."

Shay studied the insurmountable wreckage of the collapsed tunnel and the fallen fire engine with a desperate gleam in his eyes. "We can't get past this. Unless we swim." He stared at the sewer waters, frowning. "Something tells me that if they catch us in the water, we won't stand a chance to either flee or fight."

Dev nodded. He'd already reached that conclusion on his own. As long as these secret passages connected with the sewers, they were in danger. As far as he could tell, they had only two options, one of which was a guaranteed suicide mission. "We have to get back up to the surface. If we stay down here, we're at a disadvantage. I hope the fog might provide us with some cover."

"How're we going to get back up to the streets?" Shay asked, still anxious. "We find a new manhole, maybe?"

The idea was good since it was likely there'd be several manholes littering the streets. But the suggestion also implied they'd be spending far too much time down in the sewer tunnels searching for an exit. To Dev, that wasn't acceptable, as that move risked their lives needlessly, considering they had an unguarded opening directly above them.

CLIMBING THE truck took a lot of time, several attempts, and considerable acrobatics on the parts of both men. Obvious avenues of advancement turned out to be dead ends or were blocked by unseen rubble or wreckage. But they eventually found a way. When they finally reached the ground above, they both landed on the dirt on their backs, heaving and sweaty.

"Let's… never… do that… again," Shay mumbled through harsh gasps.

Dev agreed with a husky chuckle. "Understood." He lifted his upper torso by rising on his elbows as he inspected their surroundings.

Cordoned off by tilted or broken wooden fences, the area appeared to be the fire station's backyard. Rusting pieces of scrap metal lay scattered along the dry, brown grass. Aluminum planks covered more metallic trash, nothing functioning, everything reduced to garbage and waste. The fire station itself had partially collapsed into the gaping ground, while a couple of bare structural elements and sections of the roof remained, hanging on by a thread. One storm and the rest would be dust. A single fire engine stood in its bay, the cover dented and torn, red paint chipped and flaked. The tires had been slashed, either by the raging decay or on purpose, and Dev figured the engine had either been removed or ravaged beyond repair.

The place was utterly abandoned. No sign of anyone having been here in ages. Best of all, the fog hadn't dissipated but lingered close to the earth in a thick gray wall.

Above them rose an endless expanse of starry skies. Night had fallen. The mist didn't reach very high, though, leaving their view of the heavenly arch unobstructed. It was a peaceful sight to behold.

Dev was too cynical, however, to have faith in the idea that these Innsmouthian folk slept during the night and therefore wouldn't bother to search for their escaped prisoners. No, Dev and Shay couldn't afford to stay in any one place for too long. Nowhere was safe.

Having caught his breath, Dev stood, his muscles protesting and causing him to groan. "Come on, Shay. We'd better get a move on."

He kept his voice low in case anyone was hiding in the shadows. But he knew the precaution was ridiculous at best: If their enemies approached, they wouldn't do so quietly or subtly. They would merely count on their superior numbers, strength, and speed, and kill Dev and Shay as soon as they got their hands on them.

Then they heard a sound, unlike any they'd heard before. A continuous flow of low tones danced in the air.

Dev stared wide-eyed in the direction of a dark, narrow alley where the beautiful noise seemed to come from. "What is that?" he asked, whispering because he didn't want to disturb that ethereal sound.

Shay moved to Dev's side, and he too was holding his breath to listen better. "I… I think…. Yes, I think that's… music."

Dev turned his gaze to Shay, confused. He didn't know that word. "What is music?"

A pensive, focused look rose on Shay's face, one that told Dev that Shay was busy trying to recall something he had learned.

"Music is an art form," Shay finally murmured, awestruck. "It is made with musical devices that produce sounds, or vocals, or a combination of both, to create a… a mixture of sound and silence, a rhythm of notes strung together to generate songs and—"

"So music is like singing?" Dev knew about singing. A couple of people in Canal City could sing. But he hadn't known all of it was called music. It wasn't a word an airship captain had much need of in the performance of his duties.

Besides, of all the places in the world, Dev would never have imagined hearing music in a ruined seaside town filled with alien monsters.

"It's beautiful." Dev could confess the truth of his emotions not simply because of his present company, but because the experience overwhelmed him and filled him with a kind of hope he had never felt before.

"Yes, it is." Shay sounded exalted and sad at the same time. Dev understood. In the song, a woman sang words in a melancholy tone about pyramids along the Nile and sunrise on a tropic isle. The overall mood glided on feelings like longing and lovers far apart while the haunting rhythm beneath the voice spoke of soul mates who belonged together, no matter the distance.

"But where is it coming from?" Dev asked, bewildered. "Considering these fish men we've seen, I can't picture any of them being able to… to…." The right words escaped him, for he had no knowledge of them.

"To wield or play musical instruments?" Shay finished softly for him. Dev smiled in gratitude and relief at knowing it was of no consequence that he couldn't find the correct phrases. Shay wouldn't mind. "Neither can I. They don't seem dexterous or inventive enough to produce beauty in any form, let alone music." He glanced at Dev with barely concealed enthusiasm. "Should we go take a look?"

Surprised, Dev considered refusing Shay's suggestion. After all, the music seemed to originate from the south, which would take them in the wrong direction. On the other hand, his own interest had been piqued. Since the Innsmouthian people they had met appeared incapable of emotional displays of any kind, perhaps the music Dev and Shay heard indicated the existence of people that weren't horrible alien monsters bent on world domination.

"Malia gave us a strict order and a narrow window of opportunity to get ourselves out of harm's way," Dev reminded Shay, fulfilling his role as the voice of reason despite the temptation to satisfy his curiosity. "We shouldn't delay."

"But there could be survivors," Shay pointed out, "who aren't like the ones we've encountered. If so, shouldn't we at least take a quick look? Isn't that still part of our mission? It won't take long, I'm sure."

Dev hesitated a moment, but Shay made a compelling argument, especially when Dev's own inclination was pushing him in that direction. "Very well," he agreed. "We'll check it out, but it will have to be fast."

Shay nodded, appearing more innocent than usual with his bright blue eyes and his pink lips that twitched with a pent-up smile. "Fast as lightning, I swear."

Dev harrumphed and rolled his eyes. But he wisely left his opinion unsaid. Shay's inquisitiveness had gotten them into adventures before, though nothing as sinister as the one they were enduring at the moment.

Between a tilted wooden fence and another smaller building to the west ran a small alley. Dev crouched and snuck into the shadows, Shay hot on his trail. The wretched, tight space was littered with waste: wet newspaper stacks turned to unreadable pulp, wood boxes that functioned as trash receptacles, rusted tin buckets containing the remains of rotted fish skeletons, and pools of chunky liquid that could have been mudded rainwater, piss, or vomit.

Dev shuddered and nearly gagged. He had to cover his mouth and nose to prevent the disgusting fumes from making him lose his stomach contents. Behind him Shay appeared to be in much the same condition.

As Dev peeked around the corner, he detected that the music was emanating from a large building across the street. Glancing at the sign on the wall of the structure they hid behind, Dev saw this was Paine Street. The words meant nothing to him. His instincts were on high alert, and he couldn't spare brainpower for anything other than survival.

The large box-like Georgian house had four floors and seemed to be in great shape, all things considered. Its gambrel roof with gables at each end didn't sag, nor was it missing any sections. Not a single wisp of smoke rose from the chimneys, but Dev could see roaring flames in fireplaces through the tall rectangular windows. Curved plaster decorations and a once-whitewashed balcony appeared above the front doors, supported by columns that had also once been white.

A fancy plaque said Gilman House Hotel.

"Look. There's a big backyard." Dev pointed at a shady walled-off area to the west. "We can get onto the grounds and inside through there. Follow me closely."

Without working streetlights and with the inclement nighttime weather, the street was cast in impenetrable shadows. The fog concealed the rest, and each end of the street vanished into gray cloud, obscuring whatever lay farther away.

Glancing warily in both directions, Dev stooped low and skulked over to the other side, with Shay again close behind. A broken section in the stone wall allowed them entry to the backyard of the hotel with an easy climb and a hop to the ground.

An overgrown garden with sickly or dead grass, plants, and trees did in no way invite leisurely walks through the park. The garden was surrounded with other structures, all of them in a state of disrepair—huge, lumbering black shapes that appeared to tilt precariously in their direction, in danger of imminent collapse, threatening to box them in without a discernible means of escape.

Dev had never enjoyed feeling crowded or surrounded. In an environment that seemed to be closing in on him, he started to feel claustrophobic. Shay had once explained the meaning of that word, and it had described Dev's state of mind quite well. Shay had postulated that when Dev was flying high in the air, surrounded by nothing but blue skies and white clouds, he could feel free of those unpleasant sensations, and maybe that was why Dev became a skyship captain.

Standing now in the wide garden space and still feeling trapped, Dev had to agree with Shay's interpretation. Right then he would have given almost anything to break free from the gloomy ambience threatening to suffocate them.

The music had grown louder. Many of the windows were open a crack or shattered. Shards of glass clung to some of the windowsills or lay scattered among the bushes at the building's foundation. Candles and gaslights flickered inside, a warm yellow glow that created a sense of welcome for the first time since they had stepped foot into town.

"The ballad is beautiful," Shay whispered, conjuring up another word Dev didn't know but that seemed to fit the… music. "But I doubt there will be much to uplift the mood in there. I just hope any potential survivors won't be inclined to kill us."

Dev nodded. He brought his rifle up and stealthily moved toward the double back doors inset with the remains of fine beveled-glass windows. Both were ajar, one of them hanging precariously on a half-loosened hinge, and the lock and handle were covered in rust. Dev gently pushed the leftmost door open enough so they could slip in. A sharp creak heralded their entry and their boots crunched broken glass. Yet no one came running out to meet, greet, or murder them.

Inside, a lavish hallway spread straight across to the right and left of them. The air reeked with a stale and musty stench, and specks of dust danced before their eyes. Critters invisible to the naked eye made noise inside the walls, continuous scurrying and scratching sounds.

Though the interior appeared luxurious, the actual structures had to be riddled with holes, eaten by worms and cockroaches and who knew what else.

Dev shuddered at the imagined visual, disgust creeping up and down his spine. "It's a miracle this place hasn't caved in yet," he commented dryly.

"Agreed." Shay scrunched his nose and pursed his lips, clearly repulsed but looking incongruously appealing anyway—at least in Dev's opinion. Shay really had no talent for keeping his thoughts and emotions a secret. Dev couldn't help but be even more enamored with the young scholar.

Thick wall-to-wall carpets, covered in an equally thick layer of dirt and mildew, muted their footsteps as they sneaked to the left hallway, toward the source of the music. Black mold grew on the walls, cobwebs spread wide in every nook and cranny, and in the corners shone bioluminescent mushrooms in tiny clusters, their green glow eerie and disturbing.

Obviously no one maintained the hotel's interior. No maids kept house here. It was a stark reminder that despite the entrancing music, their surroundings were anything but normal.

A junction led them to an area that was shrouded by deeper shadows as a result of an intense light glaring from up ahead. A staircase disappeared to their left, apparently leading to the upper levels. Wooden paneling on the walls had broken off, leaving only a few planks behind. The banister was missing several spokes, and the velvety carpet appeared as filthy as the ones they had seen before.

"We could gain a better vantage point from upstairs," Dev suggested, nodding toward the staircase. "The music seems to be coming from the front of the building. Fancy hotels, from what I've gathered, usually had some large spaces there. The foyer and reception area, a dining area, some kind of lounge and bar, and possibly even a ballroom."

Shay regarded Dev with surprise. "I hadn't pegged you as having an interest in architecture. How useful. And kind of cute." His irreverent smirk took away the sting of being referred to as cute from Dev's masculine ego.

"The second book I ever read was a manual of architectural styles." Dev shrugged, but he was secretly pleased that Shay had noticed—and that perhaps Dev possessed information unlike any Shay had. It made Dev feel like the king of the hill—or at least the king of this hillside town.

Being of the same mind, they climbed up the stairs to the second floor. As Dev had suspected, a hallway open on one side crossed above the foyer area, forming a balcony. The hallway extended farther in the direction the music seemed to be coming from. Decorated wooden pillars and beams gave the ambience a touch of warmth, and watercolor paintings on the inside wall depicted lush, vibrant landscapes, creating a total contrast to the general creepy atmosphere of the town.

No one appeared to stop Dev and Shay, or even observe them, as they sneaked toward the sounds.

Once they reached the corner of the hallway, they crouched down behind the balcony railings and peered through the rungs. They had a perfect view over the lounge and its occupants.

Velvet settees and upholstered sofas, gleaming credenzas and closed bureaus, leather ottomans and wooden coffee tables dominated the large open space, which reached a full two stories and was lit by two huge chandeliers. These illuminated a room filled with people, some of them shifting about in pairs in the center of the room, holding on to each other.

"What are they doing?" Dev asked, puzzled, his head cocked as he tried to make sense of what he was seeing. The embrace seemed intimate, somehow—two people with their arms around one another, staring into each other's eyes.

"I think that's called… dancing," Shay replied in an astonished whisper. "That must be why they're playing the music. In order to dance."

Dev shivered, this time with heat. He wanted to recreate that intimate tableau with Shay, to be able to hold him close, gently rocking to a rhythm from the past, back when the world had not yet fallen to disaster. A small warm cocoon of togetherness with the man he loved. Why had that idea been so hard for pre-Cataclysm people to understand?

"Dancing…," Dev repeated softly, imagining himself embracing Shay under mellow lights, perhaps under the stars. He hadn't known people could move like that—together or alone. Here was yet another aspect of the world gone by that he had no knowledge of but wished could be brought back. It seemed like fun, full of light and life and love. Beautiful.

"We've lost so much," Shay murmured, his tone tinged with longing. Dev was certain the comment was rhetorical, spoken from somewhere far away, a land of daydreams, fantasies, and hope. Yet he was shaken by how Shay's words echoed what he had been thinking.

"It's true," Dev admitted. "But we can relearn certain things. Like this dancing. I think I could… do that with you."

Shay didn't turn to face Dev, but Dev saw his profile, the smile curving his lips, the reddening of his cheeks, and the endearing fluttering of his eyelashes. "Thank you, Dev. You never fail to bring me hope, even at our darkest hour. You're my hero."

This time it was Dev who blushed. Surely Shay was exaggerating? But Shay's admiration gave Dev such a good feeling, he refused to dismiss the notion completely. To know you were exactly what someone else wanted and loved was a heady sensation. How lucky could a man get?

"Look." Shay pointed down to the corner of the lounge where a wooden box with a turntable, a black disk, and a movable amplifying horn sat on a sideboard. "That's where the music is coming from. I remember reading about it. It's a… a… a gram… a phone… a gramophone. No, a victrola. A hand-cranked machine that plays sounds with the help of a needle on that black disc turning on the table."

Dev barely recognized any of the words coming out of Shay's mouth. "Gramophone" and "Victrola" were words unlike any he'd come across. Amplifier, however, was something he understood in his profession as an airship captain. Nonetheless, it all sounded so fascinating. A machine whose sole purpose was to create… music? It boggled Dev's mind. In the post-Cataclysmic world, only essential devices and useful machines were constructed; everything else was relegated to the status of flights of fancy, dreams from a different time.

"It's amazing." Dev had to grant Shay that. Even one of those machines could bring so much joy to the survivors in Canal City. "We should try to build one when we get back to Canal City. For…

morale. Simply to remind us that as humans we're capable of more than destruction and basic subsistence."

Shay leaned into Dev with a satisfied sigh. "That is a lovely sentiment, Dev. When we get back home, I'll write up the proposal myself."

That evocative image of the future, crystal clear in his mind, brightened Dev's dismal mood considerably. Then he told himself to focus on what mattered. They had now discovered the origins of the music, both the people and the machine called a victrola.

But there was much more to explore and examine.

"Their clothes are odd," Dev remarked.

The women wore high heels, silk stockings, and colorful, slinky knee-length dresses that sparkled with sequins and studded gems. Their hair was cut short and dressed in crisp waves. The men wore short suit jackets, narrow trousers or short knickers, and bowler hats, giving off a casual air. All of the people had multiple vertical, pitch-black striations running down their clothes.

From their vantage point, Dev and Shay couldn't see as much as they had hoped. The women wore black lace veils to conceal their faces, and the men seemed to be staring down most of the time, the brims of their bowler hats camouflaging their expressions.

The peculiar fashions spoke of ages long gone, not the years just before the Cataclysm.

"You're right," Shay confirmed, frowning. "Their attire doesn't resemble any of the pictures from the time immediately prior to the Cataclysm. No, it's… much older. Quaint. I wonder…." He harrumphed in a hushed voice. "Until now I would never have thought that books on fashion might come in handy during our missions."

Dev noticed one other thing. "Look at the pairs that are dancing. They're not just a man and a woman. Some of the couples are two men, others two women. Is that… normal?"

Hearing the words from his own mouth made Dev uncomfortable. He didn't think there was anything inherently wrong with him because he was attracted to his own sex and had fallen in love with Shay. He wasn't an expert on normality, certainly, as that wasn't a topic of much interest after the Cataclysm. Survival was vastly more important.

Yet Dev *had* said the words. Why he was paying attention to the matter now puzzled him greatly.

"Nothing about this town is normal," Shay replied dryly. Then he regarded Dev with mild amusement and a quirked eyebrow. "As for two men dancing together, that's perfectly normal in every sense."

Dev smiled back, relieved. "True."

Shay didn't look away but studied Dev closely until Dev squirmed. Then Shay asked, "When you awoke after the Cataclysm, did you always know you liked boys more than girls?"

Dev went rigid. He wasn't ready to have this discussion now, in a hostile seaside town where they were pursued by horrible alien creatures. "Yes. Right from the start," he admitted after a moment's pause. There was no reason to lie. This was who he was. And Shay was the same, like him in every respect that counted. "I slept with one woman, many years ago. It was wrong. None of it felt right. But men? Good every time."

Shay frowned, seeming angered by the response. But then his brow smoothed, and he blinked several times, swallowing hard. Perhaps he didn't want to be angry—or, could he possibly be jealous?

"I don't know what love is exactly." Dev spoke in a rush to get ahead of anything that Shay might say. "But I know I have never felt it… until I met you." Dev stared with no small amount of glee at Shay's shaky smile and darkening eyes. "Love… I would die without you. That's what it feels like. As though I can't breathe when you aren't near. Like the world has gone dark and you are the only light left to warm me up and guide me on my path."

Shay smiled then, a big, genuine gesture that told Dev everything he ever needed to know about love.

"Yes," Shay agreed. "Like it's winter, cold and dark, when I'm alone. But when you're there, it's summer, warm and bright."

Dev leaned in and stole a kiss from Shay's plump lips. Would that he could take the time and fully indulge in the luxury of kissing the man he loved. But they were running from the villains in hostile territory. Bad timing for good loving.

With a sigh, Shay pulled back and rested his forehead against Dev's. "I haven't been with anyone other than Malia. But I never dreamed of her the way I always seem to have dreamed about you." Gently he caressed Dev's cheek and jawline. "As for what's normal, we live in a world devastated by the Cataclysm. It no longer matters when two, or more, people come together, or how they are in private. There is no one left who remembers why it was so important to care what two grown men or women did together, naked in their private moments. This issue of… orientation."

Dev frowned in confusion. "Orientation?" He was relatively sure he had heard that term before. But he couldn't recall when or in what context.

Shay nodded. "Yes. That is what it is called. Sexual orientation. Some are attracted to the opposite sex, others to the same sex. Men to men, women to women." Shay worried his bottom lip, a gesture Dev identified as vexation. "The world before the Cataclysm was dangerous for us. For gay people, I mean. Men who loved other men. But… there was light too. We could have gotten married if we'd wanted to."

"Married…," Dev repeated the word, tasting it on his tongue, testing it in his heart. "Is that like… companionship?"

Shay chuckled softly. "Yes. A formal, institutionalized version of companionship."

Dev shrugged. He wasn't averse to the idea or the practice. To him, it just seemed unnecessary because if he wanted to be with Shay and Shay wanted to be with him, whose business was it but theirs alone?

Shay grinned. "You're easy to read, Dev. Perhaps marriage doesn't matter anymore. A piece of paper in a world where few know how to read or write. My point is that since we forgot hate, we can now say, in a sense, that love triumphed in the end."

Dev considered the words carefully. "The world didn't end because of people who loved but because of people who hated. It's kind of funny how humanity had to forget who they were before they could let go of hate. In my opinion, our past is all the more reason to fill this new world of ours with love."

"The past was a heavy burden on our shoulders, yes," Shay said pensively. "Now we have a chance to rebuild the kind of world our forebears could be proud of. Humanity endures and love prevails."

Dev rubbed his nose against Shay's. "You're such an optimistic, romantic sap."

Shay wrapped his arms around Dev's neck, squeezing hard, as though he wasn't ready to ever let go. "Hah. Like you aren't, my brave, strong hero."

For Dev this bittersweet moment, being with Shay even though they were in harm's way, was as close to pure perfection as he could ever have imagined. He wound his arms around Shay's waist and held on, his instincts telling him to keep this man around for the rest of their lives. His heart swelled with pride knowing Shay loved him and with adoration for the finest man in the world.

A polite cough from nearby broke the silence, startling both men apart as sheer horror and panic overwhelmed them. Apparently death had the manners of a gentleman.

CHAPTER 9

"COME WITH me, my dear prodigal sister," Nyarlathotep said as he gestured toward the black pool of the portal's energy. "It's high time you see your home again."

Malia said nothing. Without hesitation she stepped through the portal.

Rough autumn winds blew her clothes about her as she stepped onto the rocky reef. At her feet lapped restless ocean surges. This was no sandbar or coral reef, but more of an outcropping of bedrock, jutting upward from the sea in a smattering of stones smoothed by the sea, fused together by ocean salt, erosion, a variety of windswept plants, and even a mangled shipwreck on the northern peak.

Devil's Reef. That's what this lifeforsaken shoal is called.

Far to the west, land rose from the sea in a picturesque vista of misty green and gray shapes, including the fishing town of Innsmouth. So close, yet so far. Only a few twinkling lights here and there were visible amid the vague forms of barely erect, worm-eaten buildings with their tilted steeples and sagging roofs. No wisps of smoke, no excited movement, no signs of life anywhere.

A dreamlike vision of a town, Malia concluded, smiling inwardly, for she had plans.

"Did you ever imagine seeing Innsmouth alive before your very eyes?" Nyarlathotep asked behind her. He was pleased though the nuance was scarcely discernable.

"No." Malia spoke the truth. Not that her companion of the hour would have been able to tell the difference. But her secret designs necessitated a show of trust. "What you've accomplished here is remarkable, quite a feat of creativity. Even if it is a mere shadow."

Nyarlathotep snorted. "More than a shadow or a fantasy. More than a dream."

Malia shrugged, feigning nonchalance. "Not yet." With a knowing smirk, she glanced at the tall, dark man over her shoulder, letting him in on her cynicism. It would be up to him to cast those doubts aside—and simultaneously reveal as much as possible about his long-term agenda. "You need humans for that. Their dreams fuel this… fantasy."

Nyarlathotep chuckled. "For eons we have prepared for this day, for the time when all of humanity would succumb to us. Our moment of victory is at hand."

"At tentacle, to be precise." Malia grinned at him, and Nyarlathotep chimed in with a chuckle. Yet it was not a sound born of true joy. He and his ilk were far too cold for that. "I have to admit, what you did to Lovecraft and Derleth back in the day…."

Nyarlathotep beamed, clearly swayed by praise on some egotistical level. "The Key of Condensation gave them horrific dreams and bouts of endless creativity. Those visions, as shared in literature and art, in turn created powerful evocative imagery—which is now buried in the human collective subconscious." Malia waited patiently for Nyarlathotep to continue his exalting soliloquy, and she wasn't disappointed. "Deep-ocean creatures, intelligent monsters, ancient underwater cities, terrible evolutionary turns, darkness leading only to madness. The dreams we inspired reminded humanity why they should fear the dark; not because their predators were stronger, but because they were also smarter. An alien intelligence from beyond the black stars, one hell bent on corrupting the world into insanity, slavery, misery, and death. The Cthulhu Mythos—living and undeniable."

Gazing at him, Malia purred inwardly. Apparently males were the same in any species, with a tendency to ramble on about their accomplishments and conquests. Nyarlathotep wanted to be a victor; the dreadful dark god wanted to be worshiped. Without the twist of pure evil, he would have been similar to any human males Malia had encountered in her travels, at least those before the Cataclysm. She relished his pattering on without end, speaking of achievements yet to be realized.

Finally Nyarlathotep quieted. He glanced at Malia with a gesture that might have been described as an affectionate smile had she not known better. Behind his mask of charming manners and pretty speeches lay a stark, icy interior that would never change.

"Come." He extended his hand, and Malia accepted it, saving her shivers for a later date.

Nyarlathotep straightened his other hand out before him, palm first, as though to touch something indiscernible but real. A light began to shine, bright as sunshine. Like double doors sliding open, the veil of invisibility parted. The mouth of a tunnel burrowed diagonally downward into a hollow pitch-blackness in the bedrock of the reef.

Freezing winds swept up to greet Malia, their kiss biting. What she took note of was not the expected odor of rotten fish, but the absence of all scents. She felt like she was stepping into a lightless void where everything she'd known or sensed as a human was obliterated.

For her, this place was oblivion.

"Come." Nyarlathotep pulled at her hand. "Y'ha-nthlei awaits."

As she crossed the threshold, Malia caught the glint of gold from the corner of her eye. The reef was littered with gold coins from ages ago. *Fool's gold.* Malia smirked. Nyarlathotep had really taken the story to heart, remembering to scatter around clues to the forgotten lore of times when the Deep Ones had given fish and gold in exchange for human sacrifices and mates.

Another nail in their everlasting coffin, she decided.

The underwater tunnel was cold and wet. Ice-cold water dripped from the roughhewn ceiling and along the rugged stone walls. Their slow descent along the slippery and slick, shallow and narrow, corridor was precarious at best, at least as far as Malia's boots were concerned. Then again, the place had been designed for entirely different kinds of beings, the likes of which slithered along in shadowy, cramped, underground and underwater places, slimy and scaly and crawly, using tentacles and claws to pull their weighty carcasses forward....

"You must be thrilled to see home again," Nyarlathotep said, trailing after her.

Y'ha-nthlei is not my home. "Yes," she said in a bland voice. "As much as our cold-blooded hearts can rejoice and feel the elation of walking in the deep-sea gardens."

Nyarlathotep let out a bark of laughter. "Your sense of humor has retained despicable cynicism from the humans, I see. Have no fear. You'll be purged of all alien influences."

No, Malia concluded sarcastically, that didn't sound ominous at all.

THE LIGHT at the end of the tunnel rippled. To Malia, it didn't feel like light. And yet the increasing illumination seemed to contradict her instincts.

Their journey down the tunnel had taken hours. The tendrils of frustration began to tickle Malia's awareness and claws of impatience gnawed at her resolve. But she kept a tight rein on them as the finish line was in sight.

Without fear, Malia took her last steps in the creepy corridor and stood at the precipice of the great undersea city of Y'ha-nthlei, the birthplace of haunting dreams and nightmares.

As though constructed with colossal skeletal remains of whales, expanses of curved and arched columns pushed outward from a massive central pillar that apparently housed the main palace. The whole structure resembled an autumn tree, with its barren branches expanding from the tall tree trunk to cover a larger area.

Like a delicate silken veil, an energy barrier rippled and waved down from the fragile-looking branched columns till it reached the ocean floor. Cosmic colors pulsed and oscillated in this intricate energetic web. Was it purely ornamental, or did it keep the sea at bay, creating a pocket of air underwater? Malia didn't particularly care.

The autumn tree comparison only rose to the forefront of her mind because the ruling season was fall. But to another, more sinister, part of her, the structure evoked the image of a giant spider, its legs spreading from the main body, watching her every move with a thousand eyes—ever vigilant, eternally evil.

Ignoring any annoying similes her mind conjured, Malia contemplated the undersea city of Y'ha-nthlei. A cold spark in her soul ignited into recognition, a frigid star burning alone in a blackened night sky. She knew this place. Familiarity pushed its way into her conscious mind, whispering ancient secrets to her, reminding her of her dastardly origins.

"Glorious vista, isn't it?" Nyarlathotep asked. She felt him standing at her side, like a shadow darkening her light, exuding maliciousness and siphoning her humanity with every word spoken and each step taken. "Home." He gestured her yet again to follow. "Come. Master Cthulhu eagerly awaits your report."

Malia buried the burning hatred and venomous disgust deep within her. Treasuring the fires they blazed in her heart and soul, Malia vowed not to forget who she was. And that no matter what these deep-sea creatures said, she was human. A hybrid, yes, twisted and morphed to serve purposes not her own nor of her own volition. But… she was human too.

From the viewing ledge, the narrow serpentine path took them down to the ocean floor. Malia soon realized she was still breathing air and not water through gills. Instinctively, her fingers clasped her neck. Nothing webbed, nothing moving, nothing flapping.

Nyarlathotep glanced at her, laughing. "The gills take time to form. Hence this tunnel of breathable oxygen." His hand swept about, indicating the fact that though they had emerged out from the stone tunnel, an invisible energy tunnel continued over their heads. The cold Atlantic waters didn't so much as brush against them.

As Y'ha-nthlei grew bigger in her sight, confirming their approach, Malia knew she was quickly running out of time. If she was going to make use of this small window of opportunity to gather more intel, she'd have to start now.

"Once the airships from Canal City arrive, what's next?" Malia surmised there was no harm in asking. After all, she was one of them. At least from a certain point of view.

Nyarlathotep gave her an odd look, his eyes narrowing. "What a curious question. You know the answer. The elderly will be granted their memories back while the Echeneci devour every trace of their free will." His gaze returned to the road ahead as he laughed low, eerily. "Of course, not all will be transformed into drones. A chosen few will be sacrificed in honor of their new gods of the sea—as feasts befitting immortal deities."

Even so deep under water, the shadow the alien structure cast was foreboding. Malia continued forward only because she wasn't ready to attack yet. In her heart, she prayed the time would come soon and not be stolen from her like these Deep Ones threatened to rob the world of humanity.

Beneath the energy veil that glowed in lush, vibrant colors through the visible light spectrum and beyond, fishy humanoids lumbered about aimlessly, with no sign of purpose or meaning. Would that be the fate of humanity should Nyarlathotep and his ilk win on this grim night? No. Malia would never allow it.

The main building rose before her, like a monstrous cylinder stretching toward the distant surface. The green, blue, and black walls were lined with obscene, undecipherable etched glyphs and markings. Peculiar bioluminescent lichen, moss, and seaweed covered their ancient, alien stonework in places, eroding through minor cracks. Lights of unknown origin and cosmic hues shimmered behind windows too high to make their sources out clearly.

A single doorway provided entrance to the structure, its swirling blackness oozing a kind of terror Malia had no name for. Like a tangible touch, it reached from beyond the darkness and brushed its cold, dead hand against her warm, lit-up soul like winter's frost crushing delicate summer flowers. An entire universe of insane horror and the doom of mankind.

Nyarlathotep entered the blackness with a determined stride. Malia followed, gulping down her anxiety at the last second. This time her eyes remained open. What she saw was so vast and incomprehensible that her mind reeled, unable to make sense of any of it.

The view had no beginning and no end in this twisted, surreal mirage of a place where the sane laws of physics bent or broke. Structures composed of an endless number of stairways with landings in between them. Marble columns that somehow held everything together and doorways opening to the star-filled cosmic unknowns.

Various indoor rooms and outdoor alien gardens. Countless distortions of perspective and dimensions that boggled the mind.

And there, everywhere, coiled and spiraled around everything, were tentacles with nothing and no one attached to them. They seemed to emerge out of thin air, dominating the insane landscape and, with a touch, controlling every aspect of it. A cosmic being, its existence a madness-inducing crime against the laws of physics and reality and nature. A filthy affront to everything benign and good and decent.

Gripped with vertigo and sensing her rational mind slipping beyond her reach, Malia couldn't tell if she was rising or falling, flying or swimming, moving ahead or standing still. The whole of the universe at her feet and arcing above her, she clasped her chest against the painful compression of suffocation. Death awaited her at each instant.

Malia cried out in the cold grips of a nameless dread. She wasn't only losing her sense of reality and normalcy; she was losing her sense of herself as a human. "*No!*" She grabbed her head, a fierce throbbing threatening to explode her brain from all the newness flooding her, drowning her.

A firm grip on her shoulder snapped Malia out of the insanity-inducing horrors.

Nyarlathotep spoke softly. "Home is where the heart is. But the mind? Ah, now that is another matter entirely. Come. Shake the lingering fumes of fantasy and insanity from your eyes and walk with me."

Getting a grip on the crazed delusions she'd envisioned was harder than Malia could have imagined. Their memories challenged her human views of what was natural and harmonic and alive and possible.

Trapped in those psychedelic visions, it took Malia a moment to comprehend they had actually stepped through the portal already. Though the new view offered more rationalities, it also evoked alien designs, an otherworldly feeling that confirmed her worst fears.

At the heart of the dead tree-like structure was a round pool. Shimmering black waters rippled as though caressed by gentle winds. But there was no breeze, not there in the underwater alien kingdom.

Occasionally a bead of liquid would form on the surface, shining like a black pearl, only to drop upward toward the unseen, shadowy ceiling.

At the center of the black pool stood a green monolith. Unlike the walls, floor, and ceiling, the smooth surface bore no carvings and no etchings. Nothing marred the silky surface that reflected every source of light around it. Malia could tell the color was green. Her brain provided her the information. Yet… her senses warned her not everything was as it seemed.

Around the pool knelt and bowed hundreds of those human-fish creatures, chanting in garbled gurgles and high-pitched clicks, creating a cacophony of unbearable noise. Whatever the monolith represented or symbolized, clearly it was worth worshiping, if these former humans were any clue. On all their backs and necks glowed an alien vampiric squid, nourished by… things Malia didn't dare to contemplate.

"And now," Nyarlathotep said in a booming voice that silenced all those present. "It is time for our feast." His hands rose toward the surface of the sea. "Raise the sacrificial altar."

It took two Innsmouthian men on either side of the pool to turn the huge wheels. From the black pool, in front of the green monolith, a rectangular platform lifted, with a metallic shearing sound that echoed through the undersea city. Grand chains appeared, hoisting the slab up from the pool where, curiously, the waters receded and parted, giving way for the machinery to elevate.

On the metal slab lay a naked figure, short and thin, with copper-hued hair and freckles on pale skin, quietly sobbing….

"*Wren*!" Malia exclaimed, her heart wrenching in her chest, aching and bruised.

Nyarlathotep chuckled. "What an ill-befitting name for such a youngling. He's far less than we had hoped for our first feast, but beggars can't be choosers."

Now Malia knew what conflict of interest felt like. She could either maintain her cover and let these creatures do what they willed to poor little Wren, or take hopeless action and save him, for a few moments at least. They were surrounded by an army of able-bodied drones commanded by a monstrous entity, and their chances—or more to the point, *her* chances, since Wren wasn't able to fight in his condition—of coming out the victor were pitiful indeed.

What in the holy hell am I going to do?

Bᴜᴛ ɪᴛ was Nyarlathotep who solved her ethical dilemma.

His voice, cold and stark, reduced Malia to fits of rage and hollow sorrow. "Malia, stay where you are. We wouldn't want any unpleasantness to interfere with our banquet." She shot daggers at him with her gaze, but to no avail. His victorious grin never faltered. "You recalled many of your abilities as a hybrid once you touched the key. Your assumption that we could not penetrate your mind once your memory was restored… well, it was correct. However… walls have ears. I must say I was terribly disappointed in you when your discussion with the prisoners suggested you had switched allegiances."

Malia spat out a somber laugh, aware the jig was up. "I never swore any allegiance to you, Nyarlathotep, or has *your* memory failed you?" The tall, dark man grimaced and growled, but Malia beat him to the punch. "This world belongs to humans. *We* are the intruders, not them."

Nyarlathotep laughed, a cruel sound. "No. We are the conquerors of this puny planet."

Malia rolled her eyes. These creatures might not be able to show affect, but were they capable of it? Could they be… provoked? "Conquer with what? Daydreams and illusions? Not exactly the stuff of legends." She let every word drip with disdain and every tone ooze scorn.

Unfortunately, Nyarlathotep wasn't rising to the bait that easily. His grin spread wide to reveal sharp fangs, too wide for mere mortal and normal men. "Humanity owes you, my sweet Malia, a great debt, one that can never be repaid." Malia knew what Nyarlathotep was hinting at. The only thing she could do was pray that Wren couldn't hear them. "We always anticipated the day would come when the arrogance and greed of humans would be their downfall."

"The humans didn't bring about the Cataclysm," Malia accused sharply. "You did."

Nyarlathotep smirked. "Yes. Or… to be precise, *you* did."

More than anything, Malia truly hated knowing she had indeed caused the Cataclysm. "They were innocent. They didn't deserve their fate. Our meddling—"

"*Pfft.*" Nyarlathotep dismissed the very notion with an elegant swish of his hand. "We didn't force the humans to use weapons of mass destruction against one another. They pushed the buttons and fired entirely of their own volition, driven by hate, greed, lust for power, arrogance, presumption, and prejudice."

Yes, that was the ultimate truth. No matter how much love existed in the world for all humans to share, someone always hated someone. Usually for no real reason at all.

Malia spat out the words like they were poisonous, like acid burning her humanity to cinders. She had to propel them aside or they would destroy her. "Yes. Humans might have pushed the button. But… I had already altered the design of their weapons. I was the instrument of chaos, doing your bidding."

Nyarlathotep chuckled. "Like I said, humanity should bend down on their knees before you, considering you spared them nuclear fallout and nuclear winter. Instead of World War III, all they got were harmless electromagnetic pulses, worldwide—"

"Harmless?" Malia growled. "Earth has been shoved back to the stone age."

Nyarlathotep shrugged, radiating indifference. "As if they ever left it. Barbarians, the lot of them." His gaze landed back on Malia, seemingly pleased, like the proverbial cat that ate the cream. "Thanks to your modifications to the global net of EMP weapons they used, not only was humanity's ability to use electricity, machinery, and technology taken from their pathetic paws, but the pulses wiped their memories as well, robbing them of their bioelectrical storage capacity."

Briefly Malia considered the possibility that Nyarlathotep and his ilk didn't understand how memories were stored in the human brain. Because she had been the chief artificer behind this coup, she was well versed in the field of neuropsychology. And these cosmic beings, the alien Deep Ones, didn't function the same as *Homo sapiens*.

Despite the actions she'd taken, Malia wasn't convinced that bioelectrical mechanisms within the brain were responsible for keeping memories stored and intact, not alone anyway. In fact, she surmised that the electromagnetic pulse weapon she had designed merely prohibited the bioelectrical or electrochemical *access* to these precious caches of memories that more than likely used biochemical means to store data.

This theory implied that the engrams within humans were still there; the modified pulse merely hindered the ability to reach them.

Not that Malia was about to share this particular insight with Nyarlathotep. If she was right—and it was still a big if since she had no way of confirming or refuting the theory—humans didn't need these creatures to restore their memories. Hopefully the memories would simply become accessible again after some time had passed. Nature's own repair kit.

In addition… she now understood why turning the people with the Innsmouth look into idiotic drones required the small squid creatures to latch on to them. Those fish-humanoid hybrids didn't completely lose all traces of the parts that made them human until the Echeneci completed the transformation by overwhelming their limbic systems and thereby extracting their emotions. Thus would their humanity be fully eradicated.

It seemed the instinctive pull toward humanity, the dominant *Homo sapiens* species native to this planet, was stronger within the hybrids—those like Malia—than Nyarlathotep and his ruling kind were willing to admit or even consciously acknowledge.

Oh, the sweet arrogance of the mighty. How they would fall.

Malia also now knew why she'd allowed the modified EMP weapons to launch: the spark of humanity within her hybrid form was absolutely more pronounced and mightier than the droplets of alienness. She was unique, not chained by either side, and fully capable of being herself and making her own decisions, regardless of Nyarlathotep.

Malia personified a watershed event.

Nyarlathotep continued on merrily, without any awareness of what was going through Malia's mind right then. "Because of your unique hybrid essence, not all of your being was erased when the weapon launched. It was unforeseen and unfortunate that you lost as much as you did of your true self. Yet your subconscious mind still retained the knowledge of your true origins, which led you here, back home."

Like a predator, Malia bared her teeth in a brash act of unbridled defiance. "This dank, seaweed-infested slime hole is *not* my home." She lifted her chin proudly, even though she suspected it might be her last act on this earth. "I'm more human than I will ever be your kind, Nyarlathotep. I will never be one of you."

With an intimidating grin, Nyarlathotep said, "Yes, you will."

Malia needed to buy time to figure out a plan to rescue Wren, so she stalled by saying, "Would I be right in assuming you and your treacherous kin have no intention of working together with the Sovereign Society either? I assume they are mere pawns in your games and plans to take over the world."

Nyarlathotep bowed his head a little, as though he revered Malia's insight. But she had a sneaking suspicion he was merely placating her, confident of his tactical superiority. "Humans don't need excuses to step on one of their own kind on their way to the top. Their pride, greed, lust—all the wonderful weaknesses they exhibit—will be their downfall. As they already have shown. This time the culprits are men and women who should, due to their advanced years and accumulated wisdom, know better. They should step down and allow others, the younger generations, their time to rule. But, as it always is with humans, their weaknesses never fail to surface. This old guard, they're slow to change and act, if they ever do, caring only for gathering plunder and harnessing power for their own good. Fools."

What could Malia say to that? Especially since Nyarlathotep was right. Well, for some of the elderly. Surely not for all. The problem was, Malia could understand both perspectives.

On the one hand, to Malia, creating an invisible line in the sand based on age to determine and judge people's usefulness was arbitrary at best. As though the fact that these people had spent their long lives accumulating knowledge and practical skills meant nothing. As though their continued involvement for the betterment of society merited being sneered at. As though they suddenly became worthless due to their age. Yes, it was ridiculous and capricious.

But on the other hand… what if the elderly were like the Sovereign Society? Believing they alone were significant in the grand scheme of things and only their contribution mattered? Deeming that they exclusively should wield control and retain positions of power? Seeing to it that they alone held the key to prosperity and wealth? Believing the status quo should never change? That was the flipside of the coin. The elderly who refused to step down and give their juniors a voice and a chance to participate—they were the root of evil. Gathering all the wealth, power, and luxuries in life, everyone else be damned. Yes, men and women like that deserved to burn.

Not exactly, Malia's moral backbone reminded her. These conspirators who planned to sell their youths into slavery, they deserved to be brought to justice and be punished for their crimes in front of the society. Death was too good for them; life imprisonment served its purpose better. At least it did in *this* instance.

"I see," Malia spoke slowly, as though her thoughts were bringing her to his point of view. "You give them what they want; in return they give you everything, without realizing it."

"Yes." Nyarlathotep smiled, as if pleased by her deductive powers. "And any potential uprising will be easily squelched. Rebels will cease their reckless activities when their loved ones are in danger and once they're hunted by their own kind. Then they'll see reason and surrender and succumb to the inevitable—*just like you.*"

ROUGH HANDS gripped Malia's arms. She fought back, managing to wiggle out of the lock. An elbow to crunch a man's nose and a fist to the groin, a kick in the shins and disorienting slaps to the temples, a punch in the jaw and an arced high kick to crush the ribs. Though she too received blows and strikes, scrapes and bruises, she did not capitulate.

She let it rip, using every one of her martial arts moves to disable the men. New ones joined in until she was knee-deep in unconscious, bleeding men. She jumped, she twirled, did back-flips and high kicks, quick thrusts and efficient parries. Whatever human powers rested within her, they sparked, fueling her cold fury into scorching icy flames that devoured her attackers.

For this time she was ready to take them on. The ambush before had prepared her for this confrontation. With a few daring maneuvers she brought them to their knees, driving fear into their hearts.

All this time Nyarlathotep said and did nothing. He stood in place, watching, his arms crossed over his broad chest, an eyebrow quirked with disdain, a flicker of a smile lifting one corner of his lips. "Are you done?" His tone suggested she was no real threat.

Malia hit another fish man across his cheek, causing the man to fumble his step and fall backward, bruised and broken. "As soon as you stop sending them to their inescapable defeat."

Nyarlathotep laughed, his black hair swaying behind him like waves. "Your stubborn refusal to accept the unavoidable was amusing at first. But the joke is getting old. And my patience is wearing thin."

While Malia had her hands full with a raging swarm of Innsmouthian men and women trying their best to beat her into submission, Nyarlathotep shifted to the platform upon which Wren lay, helpless and bound and unconscious. He seemed to glide through the air, his feet above the ground, hovering and rolling like the gray mist surrounding the town far above. In fact, his whole visage grew darker, less human, more menacing.

Nyarlathotep's braids spread around his head, a dark halo or the tail of a peacock, fanning about him till they turned to shadow and smoke. The tendrils of his hair spiked and sank deep into Wren, who cried out loudly in extreme pain. His slender body twisted and bent, unable to dislodge the coils of smoke and shadow Nyarlathotep created. The tentacle hairs slithered about, twining around Wren's wrists and arms, ankles and thighs, and sucking up red streaks of blood and blue brands of bruises. Nyarlathotep's tendrils entered each of Wren's orifices, eyes, ears, nose, mouth, navel, and… lower. The things Nyarlathotep did to Wren with his tentacles… obscene and repellent… existed in an evil world beyond description and sanity.

Malia knew she was too far away. But she tried anyway, sprinting to a run.

A new wave of Innsmouthians swerved directly into Malia's path until they formed an impenetrable wall of cold flesh to stop her advancing toward her friend. This time Malia knew she was lost. Her focus wasn't on battle but on Wren, and that distracted her. The half-human, half-fish people gripped her limbs like chains and moved to subdue her, swarming on top of her with their enormous weight, their steel-like strength, and their unshakable determination to vanquish her resistance. One by one, they piled on top of her, a mound of flesh and bone, caging her in.

In terror, Malia watched helplessly as Wren's skin grew gray and pallid and his frame grew thinner, losing mass as though Nyarlathotep was draining him of everything from flesh and blood to vitality and essence. All that Wren was as a unique human being was mercilessly devoured by Nyarlathotep, until his screams died in his dried throat, and nothing but a skeletal husk remained.

Wren was dead. And Malia was toppled and defeated.

"*Nooooo!*" Malia shrieked, entangled in the Innsmouthians who had finally shoved her on her stomach on the ground, covering her every inch to restrain her.

She shot fierce daggers at Nyarlathotep with her eyes alone while his black tentacles morphed into shadows and then back into mundane braids. His atrociously wide grin spit in the face of all that was good and living and ethical and kind. His revulsion at and rejection of those essential and fundamental humane ideals could be seen plain as day. He was alien evil incarnate.

With a solemn pledge in her heart, Malia growled, "You're a monster. I will kill you. I swear it on the life of my murdered friend. I will erase you from existence."

Nyarlathotep's eyes blazed with a licentious dark light. "Many have tried. None have succeeded." His forbidding words didn't sound like an idle threat.

But Malia didn't care about his prowess. She could only feel her own need for justice and vengeance struggling against one another in vain. To her, the two were as one.

"You're pathetic," she taunted him, even as the fish men grabbed her tight and yanked her up on her feet. "You can't even make these hybrids of humans and Deep Ones do your bidding without the Echeneci. And you really believe you've got the balls to try and take over the world?"

She laughed hoarsely due to her exertions. But battling against her captors proved to be a failure as they half dragged, half carried her toward Nyarlathotep, the platform where Wren lay dead, and the pool of black ooze.

Still she mocked and goaded him. "You don't have the guts to go to war with humans. That's why you've only ever let them become aware of you in dreams, hallucinations, and madness. You're nothing but a useless bag of stinking hot air. I'll let you draw the conclusions of that remark." She scrunched up her nose, as if smelling something nauseating.

Baring his teeth, Nyarlathotep slapped her in the face with the back of his hand. The brutal contact made her ears ring and her skull rattle like dry seeds in a gourd. Red-hot flashes of pain radiated from her battered cheek, and the coppery taste of blood filled her mouth.

Spitting blood out on the gleaming marble floor, Malia jeered, "Not much self-control, eh? Like a child throwing a temper tantrum. It'd be pitiful if you weren't so loathsome and sad."

Nyarlathotep snarled at her, grabbing her by the throat and shaking her about like a ragdoll. His voice was nothing but a low growl. "You fool. Your potential as a hybrid was infinite. Infinite! And you squander it, waste it away like garbage. Throw your gift back in my face. Tossing pearls to swine. Pathetic man-fool."

The remark only lifted Malia's spirits. Even in the grips of a monstrous entity, she let her mirth show in husky, breathless chuckles.

"So you… admit I'm… more human… than your kind…. Perfect…. Thank you." Her words were garbled due to the chokehold, but they got through, if Nyarlathotep's furious expression was any indication. His eyes flashed like lightning bolts in a storm.

"You won't get the chance to regret your thoughtless words." Nyarlathotep nodded for the men to move. "Bring her closer to her final threshold."

As the group of fish men brought her forth, Nyarlathotep gripped Wren's skeleton's ankle and yanked the dried-up husk down. It thudded onto the glittering marble floor, disintegrating into tiny piles of ashes. Soft clouds of dust sifted about until the floor emptied.

Wren was brushed away, like dirt with a sweep of a broom.

Malia wanted to scream or throw up, or both.

She locked gazes with Nyarlathotep. "You're going to regret having done that."

His alien arrogance didn't crack. "You're going to regret having said that."

With a wave of his hand, he gestured toward the black swirling pool. Malia struggled. She managed to get partially loose and swung and kicked fiercely. Her captors grunted in pain, but their hold only fastened tighter until she could scarcely draw breath and the flow of blood in her veins slowed to a crawl. Malia felt faint, her mind dizzy and reeling, but at heart she knew she'd never give in.

The green monolith towered over her. Briefly her vision blurred, and the massive block of stone seemed to tilt and tip toward her.

Her guards shoved her roughly. Lest she fall into the pool facedown—to drown… or worse—Malia stumbled so that her feet entered the black liquid and splattered it about. It covered her to the shins, but it didn't move like water. Whatever it was, Malia sensed a malevolent intelligence taking stock of her.

A hard shove from behind pushed her forward. To once more avoid diving headfirst into the pool, she floundered desperately and braced her hands on the green monolith.

A blinding flash of light speared the air and her consciousness. Malia found she could no longer move. The liquid level began to rise slowly, a leisurely torment. She couldn't detach her hands from the monolith. The appalling imagery and undecipherable glyphs glowed blue, green, gray, and black. The odors of saltwater and rotting fish perfumed the air with their noxious fumes.

Malia gagged, the sensations overwhelming, the trapped feeling giving rise to panic. She tried to yank herself free but to no avail. Instinctive fear in the face of certain death rippled through her. She doubled her efforts, yielding no reward of freedom.

Nyarlathotep chuckled, though the sound was anything but cheerful. "You will be purged from your filthy human influences. Now you will be ours in life and in death. For all eternity."

As the darkness swamped her, Malia hated that his was the last voice she heard.

Chapter 10

THE GRANDFATHER clock's chime clamored surprisingly loudly through the Gilman House Hotel. The bell struck midnight, echoing throughout the lavish old structure, vibrating inside the walls and windows—and within Dev's rib cage.

Both he and Shay stared up at the man standing in the hallway, blocking their escape. He smiled politely, his tiny round spectacles dangling on the tip of his nose. His slick hair had been combed back, he walked with a slight hunch, and his necktie was perfectly straight. But… his clothes smelled of mildew and had moth and mouse holes in them.

Worst of all, however, was his face. His pointed nose twitched ceaselessly, as did his oddly long and thin mustache. His left eye bulged and gleamed pitch-black and round while his brown right eye looked like that of a normal human. His skin was patchy, changing from pale, wan flesh to light brown fur, a hideous testament to the unnatural state of their host. Dev had never seen anything like him.

"I do beg your pardon, gentlemen," the man said, bowing from the waist. "I'm afraid I was not informed of any new guests having arrived. I was at the front desk, you see, and I surely would have seen you enter the glorious premises of the Gilman House Hotel. So, do you have any luggage?"

Dev and Shay levered themselves to their feet. Dev struggled to find the right words, but Shay beat him to it, thankfully. "Our apologies, good sir. We, uh, came in through the back garden. We didn't, um, realize we should have just—"

"Oh, goodness, no worries on that account." The man snickered and waved a hand in a vague dismissive gesture. His whiskery mustache quivered as though he smelled something. "Now, luggage? Would you gentlemen be needing a room for the night?"

Dev and Shay exchanged glances, Dev worried out of his mind but Shay apparently keeping it together rather well.

"We, uh, just arrived in town," Shay said slowly, probably to buy time to figure out this stranger's angle. "We were actually wondering if you knew the best way to, uh, leave, as we're only passing through. We have, um, urgent business back home, so we—"

"Oh my, no," the man said, shaking his head adamantly. "The bus won't be available at this late hour. According to Joe Sargent, the driver, there's a fault in the engine, so the bus is currently under repair. So, a room for the night, gentlemen?"

Joe Sargent? That sounded like a pre-Cataclysm name. In fact, it sounded like the name of a fictional character, perhaps something from one of Shay's notes Dev had taken a peek at onboard *Smoke Sparrow* and didn't fully recall. Now he wasn't sure what to believe, but he suspected there was no such person as Joe Sargent. No bus, for that matter. Was their rat-faced host making it up as he went along, or maybe borrowing a character from a story for his own purposes? Or was he caught in some fantasy that played itself out in this peculiar hotel? Dev's concern deepened.

"Could we have a look around the place first?" Shay asked swiftly. "I'm sure the level of your accommodations is high, but we, um, would like—"

"A tour of the hotel? But of course, that is easily arranged. Do follow me, gentlemen." The man turned on his heels and, with another hand wave, beckoned them to follow as he headed for another flight of stairs leading down.

Dev and Shay had no choice but to walk after him. Dev could easily have knocked the guy unconscious or even killed him. But that would probably alert everyone in the vicinity—likely with nothing but a sinister or deadly outcome.

As they ambled leisurely downstairs, Shay whispered, "Look at the back of his head. No colored lights. He doesn't have one of those squids on him."

"That may be so," Dev grunted. "Plus he's able to speak, unlike the others we've met. His skin tone is closer to normal than the grayish-greenish scales we've seen, but that fur is far from natural. No, these folks are no ordinary survivors. Be on your guard."

At the bottom of the stairs, they entered the foyer. Immediately Dev and Shay could see all the little things they hadn't been able to detect from their elevated vantage point. The wallpaper was peeling away as green slime dripped down in slow but steady streams, oozing from holes like sweat through pores. On the front desk sat a gruesome stone idol of a frog-like creature with a protruding belly, tentacles around its deformed head and forming its beard, with folded bat-like wings on its back. Blood speckled the furniture, wallpaper, and carpeting, and the stench of rotting flesh and putrefying fish was redolent. The walls, ceiling, and floor seemed to tilt or wobble, as though the hotel's foundation was set on swampland instead of solid ground.

Again, though, the worst were the people, who all stopped what they were doing and turned to face Dev and Shay. Not only their faces but their bodies too appeared horribly deformed, with pustules on their skin dripping black ooze as thick as tar. That explained the black striations they had previously noticed. Not decoration but degradation. Was it a sickness or plague? Dev didn't know, and a part of him hoped he never would.

The hotel's residents all displayed disfigured frames with bent and twisted limbs, and their faces bore signs of animals other than fish—snouts instead of noses, fangs instead of teeth, missing ears or bony spines in their place, and more than the normal human complement of eyes floating on their skin. Dev recognized features of cats, dogs, horses, chicken, geese, lizards, frogs, and even elephants since in addition to human skin, they had fur, hide, feathers, or scales in indistinct patches on their bodies.

Dev wasn't sure if he wanted to gag, scream, run, or all of the above.

"WH-WHAT ARE they?" Dev whispered. He'd gone stone-cold rigid, so panicked he feared he might go mad.

Shay's hand found its way into Dev's bigger paw, trembling the same way his voice did. "I… I think… they are, uh, *were* people.

Maybe they're people who lived in this region before the Cataclysm. I don't know how they became… like this. Some failed experiment on the part of the alien monsters?"

"But they look part animal," Dev said, his free hand resting over his stunshine gun, ready to deploy it at a moment's notice. "They aren't like the others, the ones with squids on them."

"Maybe the squids couldn't attach to them for some reason," Shay replied in a shaky voice, leaning closer to Dev as his gaze swept through the room. No one moved or spoke. The music continued to play without interruption, a lovely ballad about jungles wet with rain. "I have read two books that deal with the basic elements we're composed of. They're called genes. As we evolved over millions of years, our genome included genes from many different kinds of animal and plant species, but most often they're microorganisms, like bacteria."

"Uh-huh." Dev shook his head imperceptibly. Bewilderment seemed to be his usual state of mind when listening to scholars like Shay. "I'm going to pretend I understood everything you just said."

Shay let out a chuckle so small it sounded more like a squeak. "The squids we've seen have begun to transform their hosts toward marine life forms, such as fish. Maybe… maybe these people had too many, uh, alien—as in animal—DNA. Oh, DNA, that's—"

"I'm fine not knowing, Shay, thank you very much," Dev cut in dryly. "I'm more than willing to trust your superior intellect on this one." He was getting really nervous about these people simply staring at them, not speaking or acting in any way. But neither did they appear hostile or aggressive, so that was a positive. For the time being, anyway.

An old woman in a glittering loose dress that hung straight from her shoulders cocked her head and stepped forward. Her mouth opened to reveal a blackened tongue dribbling thick muddy liquid as she gurgled, "Ph'nglui mglw'nafh Cthulhu R'lyeh wgah'nagl fhtagn. Cthulhu fhtagn! Cthulhu fhtagn! Shub-Niggurath!"

Dev and Shay instinctively backed off, horrified and disgusted by this twisted vision of humanity. Whatever the language was she spoke, it resonated within Dev in the form of negative reactions and emotions, mostly bone-chilling dread and increased panic in the face of the slow approach of a loathsome creature masquerading as human.

"Time to go," Dev said emphatically as he pushed Shay behind him with one hand and raised his weapon with the other. "Don't come any closer," he warned the shriveled, bent old lady, who pointed a bony finger at them, slime exuding now from every orifice.

"Leaving so soon, gentlemen? But you haven't even eaten your complimentary meal."

Continuing to back away, Dev glanced at the rat-faced desk clerk, who grinned with a mouthful of yellow teeth—and sank them into a live swamp rat that wiggled and squealed a high-pitched death call. Considering his appearance, did that constitute cannibalism? Dev had no idea.

"See? Delicious." The rat-man cackled insanely, blood dripping down his chin onto his clothes and pieces of half-chewed rat meat falling onto the front desk. The dead rat in his hands twitched for a second and then lay still.

"What the hell is wrong with this town?" Dev murmured in sheer terror as his instincts cried out for escape. "Will these horrors never end? Are we cursed?"

Slowly, as though chanting, the men and women in the lounge and foyer began to mutter those horrible alien words, point at Dev and Shay as if to put a hex on them, and lumber toward them, their movements jerky and uncoordinated. Though no strange cosmic lights appeared at the back of their heads and no tentacles seemed to wrap around their bodies, puzzling bursts of light like miniature lightning flickered on their skin, and occasionally their eyes glowed yellow or green.

"What are those… flashes around their heads?" Dev asked, concerned they might be a psychic or magical weapon of some kind, new to him and impossible to defend against.

Shay had his hand pressed against the small of Dev's back, guiding him to the best avenue for escape. His alarmed voice held none of the detached scholarly coolness of before. He was clearly as shaken by the most recent turn of events as Dev was yet again their hope soured, thwarted by an alien invasion.

"I don't know. Electrical charges?" Shay sounded wild, desperate, and wholly unable to flee from their tense situation into the haven of scientific analysis.

Dev almost wanted to laugh, but it would have been hysterical and half-mad. "They've harnessed electricity?" he asked, curious despite himself.

Perhaps it was his survival instinct speaking, since back in Canal City they had yet to make significant headway into electricity themselves. The best they had been able to manage thus far was to use certain chemicals to spark electrical energy on an extremely small scale—nothing that would help them with armaments, shields, or airships on an industrial level.

But Shay sounded reluctant and impatient to discuss such matters now, which was logical, of course. "There's no evidence of that kind of advanced development or progress in this stinking town. Yes, the human brain operates with a unique bioelectrical charge. Why can we see their electrical sparks on the outside? Who the hell cares? We have to get out of here!"

Dev had to admit Shay made perfect sense, all things considered. But he worried that if he fired his stunshine gun, the resulting sonic blast would invite every alien menace from the nearby streets right to them. So he hesitated.

"You sure you gentlemen don't want some swamp rat? It's to die for." The rat-faced clerk jumped on the desk, cackling like a crazed hyena, and joined the others in the odd chanting of a language so otherworldly and bizarre that neither Dev nor Shay could make heads or tails of a single utterance. "Tea time. Everyone loves a cup of tea, don't you, darlings? Hlirgh fm'latgh ng-hupadgh ebumna. Ph'nglui shugg-oth vulgtlagln r'luh 'fhalma ng-gnaiih."

If Dev lived to be a hundred years old, he would be quite happy to never again hear those odd, grim words from an alien language that sounded like ominous warnings, curious curses, or spells to end their existence. He didn't care what the words actually meant. He only knew he had to get Shay and himself out of this hellhole.

"More of those things are coming in from the back garden," Shay cried out behind Dev, confirming his worst fears. They were almost surrounded. He didn't want either of them to be eaten by these freaks. They might not have had psychic squids attached to them, but they were mad and lost, beyond Dev and Shay's aid and an obvious threat.

"Head up the stairs," Dev growled, knowing they had run out of options. "If you have no choice, take the shot. Forget how much noise it'll make. Just shoot them."

One of Shay's hands left Dev's back, and Dev heard the tiny hum of a stunshine gun ready to fire. He raised his own arm, yanked his stunshine rifle, which was enhanced for a tighter blast and a wider range, from its sheath, brought it up, and aimed the barrel at the encroaching swarm of half-human monstrosities. Whatever had happened to them, they were beyond salvation. Nothing short of death would free them from the grip of insanity.

"Come on," Shay rushed Dev, his voice tight and scared. But he didn't run. Dev was sure he wouldn't, and Shay's display of bravery proved him right.

Then Shay fired his stunshine gun. A sharp but short-lived boom and a flash of light as bright as the sun blasted from the barrel.

The disfigured creatures that had once been human held their heads, fell to their knees, and screamed in agony. A few were thrown over the heads of others and then clear across the room. They smashed against the walls, grunting, and slid down, leaving deep and undoubtedly permanent indentations.

The stunshine gun's bright blast flooded the brain with light through the eyes, and the sonic blast deafened and overloaded the target's senses and disrupted its balance. But it didn't kill. The weapon was humane, as even the pain from the percussion wave was of short duration.

"Now that we're certain there's no one left to save in this stinking town, it's time to vacate, wouldn't you say?" Dev called out to Shay sarcastically.

Shay let out an actual whoop of agreement. "Absolutely, yes. Enough exploration. The stairs are now clear. C'mon. Hurry."

Shay's words guided Dev to the bottom of the stairs, and they dashed up to the second floor. They couldn't go left because that would lead them to the balcony above the foyer and lounge, so they ran like mad to the right.

Dust clouds arose as they stomped down the mazelike warren of hallways, unable to find their way out. The walls seemed to close in on them, the floor shook under their feet, and whatever moved above their heads inside the ceiling sent flakes of rubble and plaster raining down on them. The ethereal landscape paintings on the walls seemed to melt as black and green slime started to leak from within them. A horrible pulsing beat and an ebbing and flowing hum surrounded Shay and Dev, as though the building itself were alive and breathing around them, eager to devour them whole.

Dev had never in his life run so fast. He couldn't hear much of anything over the roar of blood in his ears. And yet he did distinctly hear the stomping of numerous pairs of feet behind them. That baleful chanting resumed, as though their pursuers weren't the least bit out of breath, and every few seconds they yelled out loud, mere crazy shrieking with neither reason nor rhyme.

"Where are you going?" Dev called out to Shay, who was running in front of him. They dashed around corners, down endless winding hallways, but seemed to make no headway. They ran up another flight of stairs. At this rate they would wind up on the roof and have no way out.

"Follow me, Dev. I know the way." Though obviously scared out of his mind, Shay sounded sure of what he was saying. So Dev said nothing more. He would have followed the man he loved to hell and back again. And… they indeed seemed to be headed in that direction.

YET ANOTHER flight of stairs, and they were on the fourth floor. Dev felt like he'd been led around in circles, and he was hopelessly lost. And the noise made by their relentless pursuers merely grew in strength.

A door opened as they were running down an indistinct hallway. Dev didn't wait. He used the butt of his rifle to knock the emerging man out cold. A wet splash sounded as the weapon made contact, but Dev didn't stop to look at what part of the man's face had sunk in—or if it had ever been solid at all. They were trapped inside a madhouse. An alien asylum of mind-boggling proportions twisted and coiled around them, tightening its grip until they couldn't advance or even breathe.

Dev already felt like his lungs had compressed to two sizes too small. Red and white spots danced in his wobbly field of vision, and his muscles protested the rigorous exercise they were getting. But pure panic endowed him with a will to live, and he couldn't stop running until they were both safe.

Another door opened, and a shrieking woman with a bulging hump, twisted arms, and nails like the talons of a bird of prey lunged for him. Dev ducked and struck a fatal blow to her nape as she tripped and fell. Dev didn't stop to check if she was down for good but only hastened his steps to keep up with Shay.

"Over here." Shay beckoned Dev with a gesture fraught with fright. He had entered a hotel room, and without waiting for an explanation, Dev made a mad dash over the threshold. Shay slammed the door shut and pushed a dresser in front of it as a makeshift barricade.

The sparse room had a simple rusty cot with a dirty, smelly mattress, a round wooden stool to serve as a bedside table, and the dresser Shay had already put to good use. A filthy carpet, more dirt and dust than fabric, covered the floor; a cracked chamber pot had been stuffed under the bed; and a simple, rusted-over metal stand held a round washbasin and a jug, both made of chipped porcelain and covered in cobwebs.

The plan seemed foolish. Instead of gaining headway on their enemies, they were now caught in a dead end, in a room on the fourth floor from which they had no quick way out.

"Please tell me your plan extends beyond this point," Dev murmured in desperation as he fought to steady his breath and rest his weary, aching muscles, "or we're screwed."

Shay offered him a shaky grin and a curt nod. "Have faith in me. We will rise from the dark, I promise you that." He hurried across the room, pulled open the window, and peered outside. Dev sensed his self-confidence and was again awestruck at the multitude of facets his beloved could display in a time of crisis. "Quickly. We must be down before they get inside this room. This was how the narrator escaped in the book about Innsmouth."

Before Dev could comment one way or another, Shay had already climbed astride the windowsill. "Lovecraft was right," Shay whispered as he clambered out to grab a drain pipe and started shimmying downward. "We live on a placid island of ignorance in the midst of black seas of infinity, and it was not meant that we should voyage far."

Dev didn't waste a breath to comment on the thought that described their plight with such deadly accuracy. Instead he shoved his weapons back in their holsters, grabbed the drain pipe with both hands, and began to scale down.

A furious pounding sounded at the door of the hotel room, and the sudden noise startled Dev to the point he nearly lost his grip. The forbidding ranting in the unknown tongue continued from the other side of the door, as sinister and despicable as before, and Dev grimaced.

"Give it a rest, guys. We got the gist of it. Geesh."

He glanced over his shoulder to peer down and see where Shay was. Much to Dev's surprise, Shay had reached the first floor, moving like a deft monkey. He was a skip and a jump away from the back garden, which, at least for now, appeared void of both occupants and lights.

Perhaps they were going to make it out of here after all, safe and sound.

Then Shay cried out, a muffled sound ending with a scuffle and rustling.

Dev looked down and, his heart missing a beat, saw the rat-faced clerk tussling with Shay on the grass and tiles of the garden. Its snapping teeth sounded sharp and loud in the night as the creature strove to bite into Shay's neck. But Shay managed to shove his foot between them and pry the thing off him.

Growling with fury, all fears and doubts forgotten, Dev pounced from the drain pipe onto the rat-man, his weight flattening the appalling creature. With satisfaction born of victory, Dev relished the crunching of bones, snapping of tendons, and splattering of blood. He yanked on the rat-man's hair and kept slamming his head against the tiles until Shay touched his shoulder and pulled him off. Nothing was left of the rat-man but a wet, broken mess, thankfully obscured by the shadows of the night and a layer of fog that had slowly stolen its way into the hotel's back garden and blanketed it in impenetrable grayness.

Dev could barely breathe. His body shook violently. His hands were covered in blood and… pieces of the rat creature's flesh. His gag reflex kicked in, and he swiveled around and threw up in the bushes. He hadn't eaten in hours, but he retched until he had nothing more to give, his belly cramping painfully.

All the time Shay's hand circled soothingly over his back, and Shay whispered sweet nothings in his ear, grounding Dev from the horrors of what he had done.

"I'm a monster," Dev murmured, his voice cracking. "I killed him. I wanted to. Is this what humans are truly like? Is this what we're made of and what we have to look forward to?"

"No." Shay's voice held no uncertainties. "You saved me, yourself, and hopefully the rest of our civilization. It was protection and self-defense. He left you no choice. Come, my love. We must still run. We're not safe yet."

Shay's encouragement and rational counsel brought Dev back from the brink. With his stomach still a mess, he wiped his hands on the rat-man's clothes, and then headed to the stone wall with Shay at his side.

Dev wasn't a fool. He would revisit this terrible act he'd been forced to commit in future years, if he lived that long. He foresaw many a sleepless night filled with nightmarish images of the rat-faced man who had tried to kill and eat the only man he had ever loved. And that creature wouldn't have done so in order to avoid starvation; he would have murdered and slaughtered for fun and for whatever dark gods they worshiped. He'd been a malignant being, and what Dev had done was a blessing on the world.

So Dev pushed the thoughts of the man he had slain out of his mind and refocused on the matter at hand, which was survival, by no means guaranteed.

Just as they stepped onto the stone fence, they heard screaming from on high. They looked up and saw a cluster of insane creatures peeking at them from the fourth floor. They shook their fists at Dev and Shay, yelling after them, one by one dropping out of sight, perhaps to continue their pursuit.

Dev had to admit Shay's plan had been a good one. They had reached the ground quickly on the drain pipe while their foes had been forced to spend their time and energy on the improvised blockade. They wouldn't be fast enough to catch Dev and Shay, who could vanish from sight merely by crossing the street.

"Let's get out of here, shall we?" Dev suggested with dry humor.

Shay chuckled softly. "Leave it to you to be succinct."

Dark clouds had passed and stars twinkled on high. But closer to the ground the mist hadn't evaporated, obfuscating their surroundings. They climbed over the stone fence and hopped onto Paine Street.

As they did so, a low howl emerged from the direction of the Gilman House Hotel. With nervousness tickling at his spine, Dev turned to see what was causing the commotion. Shay did the same at his side.

Together they witnessed how the reality, the three dimensions, the very space around the hotel began to ripple and undulate, as though the thin walls separating stable waking life from the wild distortions of the dream world had started to collapse. Black sludge poured out from the dark stone in rivulets, and a thousand round, black eyes seemed to pop out of the mire, searching for intruders. A shapeless form seemed to digest the building whole within bubbling currents of luminescent green ooze that rippled through the black mud like streams of putrescence.

"Have I gone mad? Am I seeing things?" Dev couldn't believe his own eyes, for the terrifying image of a completely alien life form contradicted everything he knew of the world and nature itself. His mind refused to accept what it saw, so insane and abhorrent that his reason warned him of delusions and mirages of madness.

Somewhere inside the changing building they heard screams. "Shoggoth! Tekeli-li! Tekeli-li!"

Shay tugged at his sleeve, trembling all over. "Dev, I'm scared. Please, let's go."

Without a word Dev nodded in swift agreement. Watching that living pool of darkness was enough to give any man night terrors for the rest of his life. But he wouldn't allow that image to persist and drive out the last of his sanity.

"Go. I'm right behind you."

They turned their backs to the horrors they had seen and, under the cover of the gray wall of fog, sprinted across the street back to the narrow alleyway they had used. They didn't stop their mad dash until they were back at the desolate, vacated backyard of the fire station. There they finally allowed themselves to collapse onto the ground, their hearts beating a ghastly beat and their breaths caught in their throats as bile rose.

To Dev's added dismay, though, seven skyships glided high above the town, emerging from the dark stealthily and silently. New ones popped in out of the blue, simply appearing until the night sky was littered with an armada of airships. Faint voices drifted down with the winds, but no one came into view.

"They've come," Dev whispered to himself in desperation. He sensed the beginning of the end growing nigh. Soon the age of men would be lost for good.

"We can't worry about them now but only about our own skins," Shay said as he sat up and stretched his arms and back, his joints popping in the quiet. "How far do you think we are from the coast?"

Dev pulled himself up to a sitting position, groaning as his abused body objected. But they didn't have the luxury of staying put too long. "According to the maps you have, the fire station is tucked between Paine Street and Bank Street. Manuxet River is directly north of Bank Street and the Town Square is to the east."

"How trustworthy are these maps?" Shay sounded skeptical, even mournful. It seemed he had lost faith in his skills at research and his self-confidence as a bona fide scholar.

"Shay…." Dev inched his way to sit next to Shay and wrapped his arm around Shay's shoulders. "Come on, now. None of this is your fault."

But Shay only looked more miserable and defeated—slumped, jaw quivering, eyes moist, voice cracking. "Coming here to Innsmouth was my idea. I really thought we'd find… something good, you know? Not abnormal alien creatures trying to change or kill us." He sniffed, wiping his nose on his sleeve, then doing the same to his glistening eyes. "We might know why the Cataclysm happened, but if we ever get back to Canal City alive, we'll be stealing hope from everyone. We can't get our memories back. Not unless we…." His voice faded.

Dev growled. "That price is too high. Humanity might never recover what's been lost. But we won't become slaves, or feasts either." He squeezed Shay gently and bussed him on the temple. "Shay, you're a hero."

Shay gave him an odd look. "How do you figure that?"

Dev smiled encouragingly because that was all he could think to do. "Without you and the decision to come here, these Innsmouthian people would've discovered some other way of using us. Because of you we know the truth about the Cataclysm, *and* we have a chance to fight against them. That means something, dammit."

Shay gave him a fond look, a flicker of a smile gracing his lips. "I don't think I've ever heard you swear so fluently."

Dev dipped down and kissed Shay, just long enough to savor the warm softness and sweet cocoon of intimacy. "I have my moments." With another swift smooch, he said, "We should get going. I doubt we have much time left before… before all hell breaks loose."

As they gripped each other for mutual leverage to get swiftly back on their feet, Shay chuckled. "I see you've been studying your idioms."

Dev rolled his eyes as he brushed dirt from his backside and pants. "If that means like phrases, then yeah, I've been doing some reading. Plenty of books on the ship. Now shush so we can get a move on."

In response, Shay playfully stuck out his tongue. Dev laughed, surprising himself how natural mirth and joy sounded, even in an unnatural, ruined town belonging to monsters.

THE SECOND they reached the corner with a direct view to the Town Square, it became obvious they'd have to find yet another route south, toward the harbor and their ship. A broken-down statue and its cracked pedestal no longer dominated the large semicircular plaza. But a mass of people gathered there, aimlessly roaming round, lumbering forward sluggishly, mouths opening and closing like fish on dry land. They seemed to be in no rush, but they also appeared to serve no function. Their movements mimicked human behavior but without purpose.

What Dev hadn't paid attention to before was now impossible to miss.

These fish folk let out almost no sounds, not even vague emulations of human speech. Either they behaved as though they were mute, or they made an odd clicking noise, combined with an occasional whistle or tiny bursting huff. None of it resembled human communication.

Dev grimaced, ice-cold shivers running up and down his spine. They had to get out of here, and the sooner the better.

They sneaked and then jogged back to the safety of the empty fire-station lot.

"Dammit," Shay blurted, kicking a loose pebble into a spin through the grass.

"I'll never tire of *your* cussing. It's kind of… hot." Dev smirked when Shay glared. "We have to remember this town is theirs, and we have no idea how many of them there are. We got only a glimpse of their numbers back at the lodge."

Shay hugged himself, appearing desolate. "That doesn't bode well for Malia. I hope she's okay…."

Shocked that he didn't feel a twinge of the usual jealousy that plagued him when the talk turned to Malia, Dev found the inner confidence and courage to say, "Malia's a big girl. Strong and smart. She can handle anything that comes her way. I'd hate to be her enemy."

Shay regarded Dev like he'd hung the sun, the moon, and the stars. Dev blushed deeply, rubbed his nape self-consciously, and cleared his throat. "There's a bridge up ahead to the west where we could cross—"

An ear-piercing squeal sounded from the shade of the fire station.

Dev and Shay damn near jumped out of their skins as an Innsmouthian man shrieked and ran toward them, lunging with his arms raised, a mad light burning in his eyes.

Dev reacted instantly. He yanked his stunshine rifle in front of him and fired.

A blinding burst of high-intensity light and a deafening sonic boom struck the man dead-on. As though he'd been hit by a gigantic invisible wave front, he blasted through the air in a high arc and slammed into one of the chipped support columns of the fire station.

A single gurgle was audible upon impact, and a stark smattering of blood dyed the gray granite red. His lifeless body slid down the column and thudded to the ground in a wet bundle of limbs, like a broken ragdoll.

"Holy… shit…," Shay whispered, breathless and in shock. Dev could relate.

An intense flash of colors like the polar lights emanated from the man. It waved about him, engulfing him. Then it dimmed, flickered, and finally went black. Both the man and the creature controlling it were dead.

Dev couldn't believe what he'd done. His reaction had been based on pure instinct. It was him or the other man. Dev had killed once before, when an expedition had turned into a rescue, and he'd been forced to slay a wildling bandit wielding a blunt club. To this day he carried the scars of that encounter on his skin—and buried inside his soul. He still wished he could have done differently.

But this Innsmouthian man's death? A slave to an intelligent, evil alien squid; a mindless drone without hope of reclaiming his lost humanity? Try as he might, Dev couldn't let go of the notion he had freed this man. Unfortunately, the liberation had come about through violent death.

If he survived this day to tell his tale, Dev had no doubt this sorry choice, like the one before, would haunt him for many a night to come.

A soul-shattering scream pierced the night. Countless similar voices joined the first in a terrifying cacophony of maddened howls.

"Dammit…." Dev sighed in anger, gripping the butt of his rifle with clammy hands.

Malia was right. Once a single one of these squid creatures died, the others became aware of the act instantly. Now the whole town would be hot on their trail. The hunt for the kill had begun.

And Dev and Shay were the prey.

THE FIRST barrage of Innsmouthians ran around the corner, their movements jerky and erratic. They swayed from side to side, hopping unsteadily. But the second they spotted Dev and Shay, their determination and speed grew noticeably, increasing at an alarming rate. The creatures would soon outrun them.

"Go! Go!" Dev shouted at Shay.

Shay skedaddled with the best of them, dashing through a hole in the fence, reaching Bank Street with the stride of a madly hopping bunny chased by a wolf. Dev followed him, jumping through the aperture at a run, feeling and hearing his coat snag and tear on the broken edges of the planks.

The dilapidated bridge up ahead to the west, a shaky wooden construction with several boards and rails missing, already swarmed with a new score of Innsmouthians, all of them headed in their direction, clearly having detected them.

All vestiges of their prior humanity had fallen off, like autumn leaves from trees. In its place were bug-eyed creatures with wide foaming mouths full of knife-sharp teeth. Their hands were webbed between their fingers, their gray skin exposed as glistening scales, and from amid their hair, fins protruded outward at the top and on the sides of their heads.

Apart from moving on two legs, they resembled fish far more than men.

Hastening his steps to reach his companion, Dev saw Shay raise his stunshine gun, pointing it at the crowd screaming and hurrying toward them, death in every eye. "No, Shay! Don't shoot! There's too many of them. It'll just slow us down. Save the ammo."

Shay growled, dissatisfied. Dev had never heard that sound before. But he didn't have time to relish its implications for his nether regions. They both scurried like bunnies, but the mass from the Town Square was gaining on them. Dev and Shay were surrounded on both sides.

In a mad rush, Shay waved toward the Manuxet River shoreline, dotted with boats of all sizes, some turned over, some in pieces, but a couple ready to launch. One could only hope at least one of them was intact and not riddled with holes.

"There! Go!" Shay's voice pitched high, scared. Dev couldn't help him now.

Shay got to one of the boats first. He kicked the stern hard, the wooden creak echoing in the air. Thankfully his foot didn't go right through any worm-eaten, rotten planks. The boat jolted forward, the bow already in the fast-streaming water. Shay jumped over some rocks—the shoreline was littered with pebbles and stones—and shoved the boat into the river with the force of his weight slamming onto it.

"Dev! Come on!" Shay leaped over the side of the boat, gripped the oars, and pushed the boat into the flow. "Hurry up, damn you!"

His voice cracked, so terrified Dev felt the sound in his chest, reverberating through his being.

Hopping up in the air, Dev whirled around and fired his rifle.

A dazzling bright light and a concussive explosion hit the closest enemy in the chest. The blast tossed his body over the heads of those following him.

The detonation blew all the others off their feet and sent them arching through the air. In unison, they yelled in agony, gripping their heads. Light clearly damaged them, as did heavy rumbling sounds. They were left on the soil of the shore, writhing in pain.

Dev was fine with that. He vaulted from the shore to the boat as it glided into the river, gaining velocity fast. Dev landed face first in the boat, Shay's hands on his shoulders, his frantic voice calling out to him.

"I'm okay, love," Dev mumbled as he scrambled back to his feet and sat on the bench. "I'm okay."

Shay hurled himself into Dev's arms, sobbing and shaking. "I thought I'd lost you. Oh, Dev, oh gods above. I thought you wouldn't make it." As Dev hugged him back, Shay's blubbering intensified. Dev had a hard time holding on to the trembling young scholar, who was evidently in shock and who took his breath away. His muttering became unclear, mostly just weeping with an occasional gasp or short cry.

"It's okay," Dev kept repeating, stroking Shay's hair and holding him close.

The Manuxet River's current was placid at first, gliding their boat smoothly along the shallow flow. But Dev felt the change before he saw the cause in the darkening night. One of the falls was upriver, but two more lay ahead as they descended in a rapid, quickening pace.

"Hold on," Dev whispered into Shay's ear as a warning. He leaned back until they both lay on their sides against the bottom of the boat. They couldn't see the falls, but the rising roar of the water was all the preamble they needed.

The boat shook and jolted against rounded rocks sticking out of the stream, the swift current driving the narrow boat along the rapids with relative ease. Water gushed against the sides, drenching them with showers of chilly droplets. The boat dove down the first falls like a piece of plywood, whizzing this way and that.

Shay breathed hard in fright, his face pressed into the crook of Dev's neck. His hands had a death-grip on Dev, who returned the favor. Briefly he wondered how foolish this choice had been. Neither Dev nor Shay could swim. Learning that skill hadn't been a priority right after the Cataclysm, and unfortunately it still wasn't. Cursing their lack of precautions made no difference now. If they survived, he would bring the necessary and vital education of the swimming skill into the Corps' agenda.

After the falls and the rough current, their ailing dinghy rocked fiercely back and forth but soon calmed. Dev didn't dare get back up since he wasn't keen on seeing either the second falls or whether any of their fishy pursuers had recovered from the shot and now chased them, swimming along the stream like sharks about to bite.

So he embraced Shay, focusing on the apple-like scent of his hair, the warmth of his skin, his hot and moist breaths puffing against Dev's neck, and his still-quaking body burrowed sweetly into Dev's arms.

Over the gush of the river, Shay quietly murmured, "I'm afraid we're not gonna make it." Dev tried to speak comforting words, but Shay pressed his hand over Dev's mouth. "If we don't, I just want you to know that you're the best thing that ever happened to me, and that… that I love you."

Shay's dulcet voice sent shivers through Dev, the kind that warmed not only his body but his heart and soul too. "I love you too, Shay. You're my heart, my life, my everything. My sole regret in all this is that we won't get the chance to be together in the dark days ahead."

Pulling back, Shay stared at Dev, their foreheads resting against one another. Shay's eyes glimmered midnight blue, his pupils wide and blown. His smile shone, even though it looked frail and small. "If not in this life, surely we will meet again in the next. As nature has shown, life finds a way to renew old bonds. So shall we, in the forever beyond."

Their lips met, soft and sweet, a mere brush of skin on skin. Their kiss was as fragile as their situation was perilous. The touch might have been faint, but it spoke volumes. Their love would endure even the most violent death.

Beneath them, the boat swayed sharply, veering off toward the final steep falls.

"Love," Dev whispered. "I'm gonna use the oars to give us some additional speed. You stay down here where it's safe." He pried himself away from his beloved and shuffled his way back to a sitting position. Not daring to look back up the river, Dev gripped and hoisted the oars over the sides.

Shay got up too, taking hold of the bow of the ship, keeping the boat level and steady. He glanced over his shoulder with a glare. "As though staying a few inches lower would make me safer than being right here with you. Don't ever coddle me again."

In spite of the madness raging around them, Dev tossed his head back and laughed.

Rowing like a man on a mission, Dev gave the oars his all, putting his back into it. Shay steered the boat by leaning left or right, depending on which rock ahead to avoid first. One couldn't call it piloting, exactly, but it was enough to get them past the rockiest shoals just before the falls.

The edge came up fast. For an instant, which seemed to last hours, time stood still as they swung precariously on the brim. Then the boat tipped over, sending them cascading down the final falls like a bird diving into the depths, hungry for fish.

The vortex beneath spun them around. Caught in a watery whirlwind, the wooden boat creaked dangerously, about to split apart. Until the swirl sent them flying off like a homing missile. Shay ducked under the bow and Dev knelt as well, hanging on to the bench with one hand and on to his beloved with the other.

Soaking wet, both men emerged to sit, coughing and catching their breath.

Squinting and blinking water out of his eyes, Dev took a look around to see where the vicious current had thrown them. Apparently just this once luck was on their side. Like a bullet perfectly aimed, the boat had shot across the bay toward the stretch of land where the lighthouse stood in its ruined desolation.

And, as Dev peered upward, he found his airship still moored to the structure.

A sigh of relief built from somewhere so deep within him that the act deflated him and then flooded him with hope and solace.

"Almost there, love," Dev said, venturing out with a grin.

With a cheerful chuckle, Shay embraced Dev from behind, wrapping his arms around Dev's waist. "Lady luck must've been on our side on this day."

"Good thing too, since we seem to be out of everything else," Dev pointed out dryly.

Shay giggled. Then the sound morphed into a scream.

The waters around them churned, bubbling about them as wild whitecaps. Huge tentacles pierced through the whirlpool, rising immensely high. As they descended, they enfolded the boat, clinging to it until the wood began to splinter with loud cracks.

A gigantic creature arose from the deep. Blinded by the showering droplets, Dev only caught vague glimpses of large, glowing black eyes, a spine and sides adorned with elongated bone spikes, an enormous mouth filled with sharp fangs and row upon row of slice-and-dice teeth, a slimy tongue, and numerous slick tentacles of fantastical proportions, covered with suction cups and claws like cleavers.

Shay cried out in terror, grabbing on to him, shouting something Dev couldn't hear.

Dev could only stare at the monster from the deep that spelled the end of their lives.

Chapter 11

SHAY'S BRAIN told him, time and again, that what he saw rising from the sea could not be real. He was a dedicated scholar, one who gave no quarter to superstition.

But as science had oft proven, there were more things in heaven and earth than were dreamt of in any single philosophy. Shay had found Shakespeare rarely required rewording, but the paraphrase fit. Science had shown that nothing was truly impossible.

Apparently even sea monsters.

The waters in the bay stormed and raged, spraying Shay and Dev with a downpour of icy shards, blinding them and forcing them to huddle close and shield one another with their arms.

Shay couldn't even recall how many times in the past day he had thought that *this* present moment would be his last. Each new occasion sucked more than the previous one. He wasn't sure how many more encouragements and last stands he could manage. Especially now, when their weapons were likely too wet to function, rendering them in effect unarmed.

Dev pushed Shay behind him and shouted through the thundering boom, "Shay, jump off the side, swim to shore, and get back to the airship. Fly out of here as quickly as you can."

Having found a rusty old harpoon on the bottom of the boat, Dev brandished it in front of him, waving it wildly at the tentacles swiping in their direction. The creature howled madly, the sound low and terrible, reverberating in their bodies and grinding through their skulls. Perhaps the noise sounded different underwater, less ear-piercing and bone shattering. Every now and then, Dev managed to cut a tentacle, sending slimy black goo dripping over them like black rain.

Shay was certain he'd never seen anything as heroic, or as batshit crazy.

"Forget it!" he shouted back to his beloved. "I'm not leaving without you!"

Was this human fortitude, Shay asked himself? Was this resilience against incredible odds? Was this a mere show of defiance against an undefeatable foe? Would this spell the end of their lives? As though the Cataclysm hadn't been an extinction-level event and a bane in their backsides already, now they had to contend with alien deep-sea monsters too?

Shay searched frantically with his eyes, discovered a fishing rod, snatched it up, and started swinging it about blindly, barely avoiding lashing out at Dev at his side. On occasion he must have hit or slapped something tangible because his hands jolted upon contact, and the monster wailed sharply and flung its tentacles off, shaking as though wounded.

But mere seconds later, a striking tendril wrapped around the fishing pole. The creature yanked it right out of Shay's hurting fingers, almost bringing him overboard along with it.

Shay fell backward onto the bottom of the boat, his head thudding painfully against the wood, sending waves of red- and white-hot pain through him. Staggering, he scrambled back up on his feet, managing to snag something metallic and sharp and bring it with him. It turned out to be a bunch of steel dart fittings for a harpoon. Yelling in rage to give himself courage, Shay tossed them toward the sea monster, one at a time. Most were deflected by the tough, scaly hide and fell into the bay waters in a hailstorm.

Seemingly outraged by the attack, as minor as it was, the creature bellowed.

Three or four massive tentacles smashed into the boat, cutting it in half, both ends starting to sink instantly. Shay screamed, then tried to take a deep breath as he plunged over the side into the churning, chilly waters. He couldn't see Dev, and his heart froze in fear at the notion of losing his one true love.

Spitting out water, he called out to Dev but heard nothing. The creature roared and stomped around furiously, if that word applied to a being that might not even have legs to speak of. Caught in the endless swirls of a raging sea, Shay kept sinking, having to again and again fight desperately to break the surface and breathe. With water in his eyes and mouth, he was losing the battle. Tentacles unseen beneath the waves swiped at him, slicing into his flesh and suctioning the life right out of his limbs.

"Dev…," he muttered breathlessly as he was yanked mercilessly into the deep blue.

SHAY GASPED as the tentacles suddenly released him and he was able to paddle his way to the surface and wade toward what looked to be the shore. A massive wave from behind him shoved him forward the last few yards. Choking on saltwater but spewing and expelling most of it, Shay lay on the pebbly beach, gagging and panting, trying to clear his head.

"Shay…." A hoarse, coughing voice close to him rang familiar and true.

"Dev!" Shay turned toward the sound and found Dev lying next to him, not twelve feet away. He crawled hurriedly to his man and lunged into Dev's arms.

The strong man took him in with ease, hugging him tight. "I thought I'd lost you."

Shay was about to declare he never could or would when a clamor from the bay caught his attention. His eyes widened at the shocking sight.

Malia glided over the surface of the water as though she were dancing on ice. She aimed her stunshine weapon and fired upon the monster, and it writhed and bellowed, huge tentacles swaying about in useless defense. Malia's laugh echoed in the winds, a sharp merry sound that spoke of victory and satisfaction, as she slid on the water that parted in her wake like two veils of cascading whitewater.

She appeared paler than usual, as a distant ice star or a haunted vision. Her eyes were bottomless feverish depths, her cheeks hollowed, her typically tanned skin now glowing as if moonlit. It was out of the ordinary. What horrors had she seen to change her so? Despite that oddness, her hair floated around her like a misty brown veil, and she moved like the wind, her exuberance dancing, buoyant, and vibrant. Undefeated.

Shay stared, climbing to his feet and wiping water out of his eyes. "Is that… is that really… Malia?"

Even if she were no more than a dream, conjured to life by his desperate yet hopeful mind, Shay accepted her presence with joy and relief.

Dev's husky chuckles sounded both incredulous and proud. "It sure is, lad." With a grimace, he cocked a thumb back toward the anchor line connecting the ramshackle lighthouse and their airship, their sole source of safety and survival. "Get up to the ship, double-time. We gotta get outta here." His gaze locked with Shay's as though knowing his every thought and emotion. "We'll bring her with us. She's our comrade after all." His wolfish grin was reassuring.

Shay leaped into action. His weapons still clung to his back, ankles, and belt, but he couldn't be certain they would still work after their dip in the bay. Fumbling slightly due to stress and weakness from the attack and the swim in icy waters, he ran toward the lighthouse.

"Wren!" he called out, seeing the rope-and-wooden ladder still in place off the side of the airship, ready to be lowered the rest of the way down upon their return. "Drop the ladder!" A glance at the wall of the lighthouse revealed they were still tethered to the ruined building. "Wren!" he repeated, louder as he fetched up beneath the ladder, which was too high to reach unless he jumped.

There was no answer from the ship above. There had to be fires burning within, or the whole construction would have come toppling down by now. Shay peered up but couldn't see much beyond the railing. Where was Wren? Why wasn't he answering?

Deciding he couldn't wait any longer, Shay jumped up and down in place until he got a firm grip on the lowest rung and hoisted himself up with grunts and burning pain in his tired muscles.

"Oh rats! I need to get out of the library chamber more," he murmured to himself as he got a good grip and managed to hoist himself up to the ladder, vowing to get into shape worthy of expeditions, the risks they included, and the rewards they promised.

Glancing over his shoulder, he watched, half in awe, half in terror, as Malia and Dev fired their stunshine guns and rifles at the massive monster from the deep sea, one working from the water and the other from land.

From his vantage point, Shay could see the creature's dark silvery eyes, big and wide as disks, its dozens of tentacles lashing about, and the silky smooth, rubbery, and scaly glistening skin that spoke of both fish and squid alike.

Was it a thing of alien beauty or ugliness? Shay shivered, unable to finish the thought.

Whatever depths this hellion had emerged from, it deserved to be cast into a deep-sea trench and buried in a hole from which it could never again climb out. For it was simply so alien and evil it could not coexist with humanity.

Grunting at his own folly, Shay resumed climbing. The ladder swung precariously in the rough ocean winds, throwing saltwater and dust in his face and up his nose, but he wasn't deterred. He rushed the last few rungs until he could grip the railing, pull himself up… and see that the deck was deserted.

No Stork, who had betrayed them for power, and no Wren, who was good and kind in a way not many could match.

But Shay didn't have time to search for their missing companion.

A shockwave shook the airship, the wood creaking, the metallic struts screeching, and the balloon above rippling and billowing. Shay was knocked back toward the railing. Without quick instincts he would have tipped overboard.

Growling, Shay got back to his feet and watched as two other scout airships aimed their stunshine cannons at the *Smoke Sparrow*, ready to fire. *My own people. How can they?* A part of Shay sought refuge in the belief he was only having a nightmare, and any second he'd be stirred awake by Dev or Malia.

But when another blast of sound and light furiously jolted the ship, tilting it almost forty-five degrees to the side, Shay was forced to accept that humans, his own people, had turned on him. It was as Malia had warned: the Sovereign Society was feeding the crews of those ships lies about Dev and Shay, with the lust for power gleaming bright in their eyes.

Shay was conflicted. Not about shooting at the other ships but about what to do with their own ship.

If he cut the anchoring tether to the lighthouse in order to maneuver the airship out of harm's way, he might not be able to swing back to fetch his companions fighting in the battlefield below.

But if he didn't cut the line, he couldn't maneuver, and he'd be a sitting duck since it took two people to load and fire the stunshine cannons. And if Shay got the ship shot out of the sky, Dev would kill him.

Six rangers jumped onto the deck, easily recognizable by their dark leather uniforms. While Shay had been busy planning his next move, a third airship had managed to fly into position above him unawares. The rangers had landed with the use of ropes; one-handed, ever vigilant, and well armed.

Six stunshine guns aimed at Shay's rib cage.

Dammit to hell, I'm sick and tired of constantly seeing my last moment on this earth.

"DROP YOUR weapons and surrender, scholar," one of the scouts shouted, his look wild and fierce, his hands shaking.

Shay knew these men, had worked with them for many winters. Soot, the mechanical genius; Goose, the naughty joker; Heron, the one with regal manners and a stout moral backbone; Hawk, the tallest and biggest fighter with an infectious, booming laugh; Dove, the swift spy and elegant social butterfly.

And last but not least, Crow, the tall Native American warrior with long black hair who radiated leadership, always in charge of a situation and his team.

"My armaments and gear are wet and don't work," Shay countered, keeping his tone level. Even if the blasted things had functioned, he couldn't and wouldn't have drawn them at his fellow companions. "Help us, please. Dev and Malia are battling that creature below. They need our assistance. They're all alone."

Hesitation flickered across Crow's handsome face, like a dark cloud passing. But still he said, "You and your crew have been declared outlaws. We have to arrest you."

Shay barked out a bitter laugh. "If we don't help our own people now, there won't be anyone left to detain." He waved a hand about angrily, pointing over the side of the airship. "Look for yourselves, damn you. Or have your unjust orders clouded your better judgment too? Are you nothing more than a bunch of feckless cowards?"

Crow's expression turned to stone. But Shay wasn't a fool. This man was honorable to the core and wise beyond his years, having been born before the Cataclysm. He dithered, conflict evident in him.

Relentless in his despair, Shay shouted, "You have been lied to. Stork has betrayed us. These creatures swore to give the elderly their memories and their power over society back. But the price is our young, enslaved and changed. If we don't act now, we will all be lost. Humanity will be a dying breed, gone before the end of the coming winter."

Crow frowned, his head cocked. He listened. His seriousness attested to it. His gaze sought answers in the others, who all hedged, uncertain of what to do. Shay could understand their ethical plight, but time was short.

Finally Crow set his jaw tight and nodded. "Show me."

With an inward sigh of relief, Shay rushed to the railing and peered down. Dev and Malia were still busy battling the gigantic sea monster. They had to be running low on ammo, Shay suspected, and their physical strength would be waning from such an arduous task. Time was running out on them.

Shay gave them a short recap of what had happened. "Stork belongs to a secret group who want their pre-Cataclysm power back. He sold us out. There's a silver key. He touched it, remembered who he was, and turned into a mindless drone, a slave. After that, he, and others who have been turned, can no longer display or express emotions. That is how you recognize them, even if they are people you think you know. There's a small creature, like a squid, embedded into the back of their skull. Do *not* let them touch you, or you will die." Shay faced Crow who took stock of the situation below with years of experience and stoicism. "We can't save everyone. But do your best to save any you can."

Crow and the others regarded him, sorrow and pain giving way to resolution and steely determination. "Rangers, fall in." His hard voice tinged with concern, he gestured toward the railing, and everyone nodded, readying their ropes to swing down.

Shay gave them his last piece of advice. "Rangers, shoot to kill. We cannot let any of them escape into the human world, for they mean to destroy us. This town and its inhabitants *must* fall." He surprised even himself at how cold and uncaring he sounded. But he knew that if he let even a single emotion burst to the surface, his precious self-control would be lost, and he'd fall down wailing and beating himself. Then he'd be of no use to anyone. "Get anyone you find up to this ship for safe haven. Save the young who have yet to be changed; forget the elderly, for they wouldn't be here if they didn't belong to the Sovereign Society. In the meantime I'll get the ship going."

"Evasive actions are required," Crow said, gripping Shay's arm before he could vanish into the bowels of the airship to ensure fires were burning. "The other ships won't fire as long as me and my men are onboard. But as soon as we hit the ground below, you're a target again."

Shay didn't have much experience piloting an aircraft, but he'd watched Dev intently enough to be able to do something at least. "I'll maneuver the ship behind the lighthouse, or try to keep something between *Smoke Sparrow* and the other vessels. But Crow? Hurry. We don't have a lot of time. This is a rescue *and* survival mission."

As Crow and the other rangers hopped over the ship's railing, diving through the air as though they were a flock of birds on the prowl, Shay rushed to see if the engine fires still burned to create steam for the propellers, thrusters, stabilizers, flaps, and wings. The steering wheel and other control sticks on the back deck ensured the proper movement of the airship. So many little things could go wrong.

The airship interiors were quiet, the wooden doors closing off the sounds of the raging battles below. The mood, as a result, was nothing short of eerie. Every shadowy corner could have held a hidden enemy, every creak might have indicated the approach of an attacker, every silence a mere calm before the storm.

Shay was familiar with all the nuts and bolts of *Smoke Sparrow*, so he didn't lose his way once. The engine room hissed and roared as machines pumped and whirled, stirring the wood-and-metal marvel to life. Everything was in working order, so whatever had happened to Wren, at least neither he nor anyone else had sabotaged or damaged the ship.

Though Shay didn't know who or what might answer, he sent a quick, heartfelt prayer of thanks to the vastness of the unexplored universe.

THE CLEAT hitch knot wouldn't open if pulled or if the rope loosened. Besides, it was their anchoring rope, so Shay didn't wish to waste it. Funny how his inner self already had prepared for a future contingency for the rope to be used—somewhere else at another time.

Keeping the rope in place, like a tether attached to a buoy, Shay gripped and spun the steering wheel, using the propellers, as well as the flaps and wings attached, to guide the ship to the east. The lighthouse wasn't very large, so the bulk of it covered only one-third or perhaps a fourth of the airship.

The rest of the fleet of skyships glided above Innsmouth. Due to their larger size and more sluggish maneuverability, only two of them were in a position to fire stunshine cannons upon *Smoke Sparrow*. They must not have had a clear line of sight to who might be onboard because they didn't fire. Could they have assumed the rangers were still on the ship?

Regardless of their thinking, Shay made sure the tether was tight as he placed the airship in a position where the ladder was concealed by the whitish-gray structure of the lighthouse. That way, anyone climbing up could do so safely. Shay prayed they could save everyone, but rationally he knew that was unlikely.

Shay dashed to the railing to peer down, scanning his surroundings, estimating he was floating sixty to seventy feet above the ground. Ascent wouldn't be easy, but staying down there would be tantamount to suicide.

As he waited, he checked his weapons. His blades and knives were fine, so he stashed them about his body. His stunshine gun gave a small spark shower, but then he heard the low-level hum, complete with a dissipating pungent smell of sulfur and ozone, plus the added effect of raising all his body hairs.

Thus rearmed, Shay decided not to wait. He had to be down there, the final guardian of those making the climb or the last obstacle for the enemy. He swung over the railing and shinnied down the ladder until he could safely drop to the rocky breakwater.

Immediately he was met with the heartening sight of young rangers and airship crews—their numbers so great that their troops had to consist of every single youth from every airship above them—fighting against hordes of Innsmouthian fish men. Clearly the jig was up, as humans had discovered their supposed new allies were nothing of the sort.

But not a single elderly citizen was in sight. They must have chosen to remain as rear guard onboard the skyships—or hiding in a hole for all Shay knew. He had neither the time nor the patience to waste on them.

Rangers had their weapons. Like scythes, they mowed through the Innsmouthian fish men, reaping bitter and bloody fruit. The stunshine blasts blinded and disoriented the enemy, but also renewed and invigorated their rage against the humans. Fumbling about, they unleashed vicious zeal on anyone they managed to grab with their hands or teeth. The moment humans were outnumbered by these vaguely humanlike creatures, they got literally torn to pieces. Violence and gore spread from the shore toward the town. Hope was a light diminishing rapidly.

"Over here!" Shay shouted across the racket of the sea storming and people fighting. He gestured for people to come to him. "Fall back now! Fall back to the ship. Come on, you runts. Run!" It didn't even occur to Shay how fast he'd picked up ranger jargon.

The closest rangers heard him and began to repeat the order with loud shouts and swift hand gestures. In a heartbeat, Shay's position flooded with escaping rangers.

"Climb up, dammit!" Shay commanded with fierce determination, part of which was sheer rising panic. "Move, move, move!"

Judging from the abject horror, flashes of pain, and grimaces of fury, none of them had been turned. One by one, young men and women clambered up the ladder, the majority spirited onward by blind hysteria. These were explorers; most of them had no firsthand experience of cruel battlefields. Not on this scale, anyway—trapped in a war, unable to trust anyone for they knew not who was friend and who was foe.

Shay kept his gun pointed at each newcomer in the continuous dribble and occasional cluster of youths as they swarmed to get away from the battleground, soaked with the blood of too many to count. These were friends and companions Shay knew.

But mostly they were people the world couldn't afford to lose if they meant to rebuild their civilization. Canal City's population alone couldn't boast more than ten to fifteen thousand survivors. Each life counted. No one could be spared.

And yet here they were, being cut down like wheat in a field.

Four or five rangers had taken up positions close to the ladder to defend the ascent, same as Shay. He was grateful for their presence and support, so to aid them, he repeated his quick recap to them, warning them to shoot to kill those who expressed no emotions or whose neck, head, or back glowed with lights and colors. It was the best and only advice he could bestow upon them without going into detail.

If they lived past this night, there would be time for true stories later.

Shay could hold on no longer. "Hold this post," he advised the others. "I'm going to help our friends on the beach. Stand fast and hold your ground. Do not let this ship be taken." Though pale and obviously rattled, all of them nodded firmly, their jaws locked, their gazes fixed. They would hold the line.

So Shay felt confident to run past the lighthouse, jump over rocks, and slip on wet grass to get to Dev and Malia. As he rounded the corner, he stopped dead, his mind reeling. He could no longer tell what was real and what… not.

CHAPTER 12

THE SEA creature had… changed. In place of the slimy, rubbery monstrosity with claws, tentacles, and teeth enough to supply a dozen creatures, rose another tentacled beast. The edges of its form faded into obscurity, like an unclear line between light and dark. This new one was born of twilight, shadows, and mist. Was this the same odious thing or a different one, propelled from the deep to squash their efforts toward freedom and life?

Neither Malia nor Dev fired at it, though. That mystified Shay even more.

The shape of the shadowy being shifted like a cloud of fog, lingering and waning, then waxing again. Shay couldn't tell what the creature really looked like.

Until it took the form of a tall, dark man with long cascading braids.

Weren't those tentacles two seconds ago?

Walking on water as though it were a solid surface, the man ambled closer to the shore where Malia and Dev stood, side by side, weapons drawn and aimed at the approaching stranger.

"You filthy misguided man-fool!" the man yelled, his glimmering black gaze aimed at Malia, as she seemed to be the sole focus of his fury. "I gave you back your memories. I welcomed you home. I offered you the chance to rule this pitiful world. And all my gifts I laid bare before you, you threw away like so much dirt."

Shay watched in terror as the man's multitude of braids morphed into shadowy tentacles, spreading around him like fog, with smoky, hazy tendrils as long as half a dozen airships, flowing about him, ready to strike here and there like serpents.

Immediately following the metamorphosis, massive bat-like wings sprung up behind his back, a shade of his true essence, casting a dark blemish upon the rippling waters.

What on earth is he? Chills clawed at Shay and his once-firm knowledge of the world.

Malia laughed, her voice strong and merry, resonating in that instinctive part in Shay that spoke of warm fires on the hearth, lazy evenings spent reading cuddled in a soft armchair, and a future so bright and joyous there was no room for fear or hate, violence or death.

"Why does that surprise you so, Nyarlathotep?" Malia taunted him, her scorn burning and hitting its mark, if his darkening growl was any indication. "Like other hybrids before me, I too played you right from the start. I was always destined to rebel. Since my initial conception, I existed solely to rise up against you and your plans to conquer this world—to mutiny, to defeat you, and to finally erase you from existence. The seeds of my revolt flourished within the soil you planted by trying to rob me of my humanity. That was the first step that has led you here, to the brink of your downfall."

Shay trembled even as he slowly, cautiously, made his way closer to Dev and Malia. He was overjoyed she wasn't their enemy, for she was formidable.

But this… Nyarlathotep? Who was he?

What he wanted, however, was self-evident, as he clearly had murder on the brain.

His arms swept in regal gestures and suddenly shot forward. Shards of ice, bubbles of water, and clouds of steam rose from the waters of the bay and moved through the air like ballistic missiles made of magic, aiming directly at Malia. Shay managed no more than a sharp gasp when these elemental projectiles made contact with her.

Only… her hand stopped them, an invisible barrier of energy between her and the odd munitions. Shay was shocked. Had Malia protected herself with some kind of alien powers of the mind? The notion seemed impossible, but her actions were there for all to see.

Seemingly unfazed his attack had been thwarted, Nyarlathotep chuckled, the cold and ruthless sound echoing along the bay. "I'll enslave this world and you along with it. Enacting an eternal torment, I'll force you to watch as I slowly slay, enslave, or drive insane every human you have ever known. Starting with that little one." He pointed behind Malia. Shay frowned and glanced over his shoulder but saw no one.

It took several blinks of an eye for Shay to realize Nyarlathotep meant *him*! Gasping, he stood frozen in place, his mind blank in fright, his instincts not yet caught up to the threat.

But Malia regarded Shay with a mere cursory glance. Then her attention refocused on their chief adversary. "No, you won't, Nyarlathotep. Do you wish to know why?"

Sauntering forward like a stalking predator, Nyarlathotep bowed his head slightly, his devious smile never wavering. "Indulge me."

Malia scoffed, "I assure you, brother, I will take great pleasure in this."

She stepped to the side casually, as though she wasn't even aware of the motion. But Shay recognized the tactic of shifting his gaze away from Shay and Dev. Shay's gratitude knew no bounds.

"When you restored my memory…," Malia began, her storytelling voice intense and captivating, a lure to the willing or the weak.

It was difficult to tell which Nyarlathotep was—willing or weak—as his eyes followed Malia. "Allow me," he said. "You recalled our kind have extraordinary powers of the mind and the flesh, yes?"

Dev sidled over to Shay, both their gazes riveted on the verbal exchange that could at any moment change into a battle of epic proportions. Without looking, Shay found Dev's hand, entwining their fingers for comfort and courage.

Malia's contemptuous tone ruled the scene. "To prepare this puny little planet for your invasion, you gave creative and artistic people the key in dreamland. Upon touching it, their subconscious minds became a nightly playground for your patient and careful thought manipulations. Glimpses of alien horrors beyond the stars, your disease spreading them through art, literature, and a culture of shared terrors that fused into the human subconscious, allowing them to thrive for eons."

Nyarlathotep laughed, slowly advancing on Malia, taking his time as she did. The two seemed to be engaged in a dance, of sorts, for superiority. Shay didn't even pretend to understand the intricacies of their relationship, but he kept vigilant, ready to spring into action.

"Yes, I have admitted this," Nyarlathotep said sluggishly, an eyebrow quirked. Shay had a sneaking suspicion this enemy didn't quite get Malia, which was why he was playing her game. Too bad for him that she was used to winning. In fact, Shay had never seen her lose.

"Just wanted to make sure we were on the same page, so to speak." Malia chuckled at the inside joke, which Shay only comprehended because he was literate and was well versed in the works of Lovecraft and others—all of which he only now recognized as fiction, not fact. "Once you had established the base of our kind into the mindset of humans, you were ready to put your plan into action. You bided your time, watching and waiting as humans brought their own world to the brink of annihilation with their arsenal of weapons of mass destruction, everyone with their finger on the button."

Nyarlathotep nodded regally, as if acquiescing to her accusations was a mere trifle. "Oh yes. With the whole world cowering in fear of tomorrow, the apocalypse of their existence, it was so easy to whisper into their dreams, fill their souls with dread, and finally launch those fearful phantasms into the world. Trapped in panic, humans did what was to be expected: They struck first. All of them. Cue modified EMPs, and—*bam*! End of the world as humans knew it."

His hands fisting at his sides in useless indignation, Shay would have stormed over to give that man what was his due if it hadn't been for Dev's strong hand gripping his arm and stopping him. Dev's glare spoke volumes. *What are you thinking? He's an alien monster!* Shay blushed fiercely at the wordless scolding, and resettled under Dev's arm, hugging himself for comfort.

Nyarlathotep laughed, obviously exceedingly pleased with himself and his triumphs. Surprisingly, Malia joined in his merriment. But her voice held only disdain and a note of victory. Shay had no idea what was happening.

"Oh, brother, if manipulating humanity's dreams is all you're capable of, the end of you is nigh indeed." Malia's hazel eyes burned with a dark flame, the kind of which Shay had only ever caught glimpses. As an opponent, she was deadly.

NYARLATHOTEP GROWLED. "I have destroyed humanity, sent them back to the dark ages. Look at all that I have inflicted upon this world and be awed and weep. Sing your last lamentations for poor humanity." His arms stretched to his sides, waving about in grand arcs.

Shay saw the fleet of skyships floating above the town, and they were firing stunshine cannons—on their own fleeing crew members and rangers. The elderly folk, most likely, making a last-ditch effort to save their hopeless bargain with Nyarlathotep. The fog had lifted from the town at last, so the view was crystal clear and stark in its brutality.

Shay suspected Nyarlathotep might have actually created the mist in the first place.

Innsmouthian men and women intercepted rangers and crewmen, or tried to at least. A lot of them fought back, with rifles and guns, sticks and stones, even their bare hands. Their spirit could not be broken, not even by alien undersea creatures instilling madness and unleashing fears upon them.

"This is only one town," Nyarlathotep rejoiced. "Soon I will spread across the globe and bring the dark glory of Mother Hydra and Father Dagon to humans. I shall win."

Malia snickered, the sound seemingly excruciating to Nyarlathotep, who cringed at the sound but still appeared more menacing with each steady step he took to get closer to her. "Humanity may have dreamed of you, brother, and of our kind. But they weren't your slaves even then. Their endurance against horrors surpasses your petty attempts. They have foiled you many a time, unseen by you through it all."

"That is a filthy human lie!" Nyarlathotep screamed. He stood a mere two steps from the shore now. The beach waters raged in his wake, his shadowy tentacles flew about angrily, and sand and dust danced around him in crazy swirls.

"No." Malia grinned then. Even from afar, Shay could tell *that* was a gesture made by a true winner. But how? Nyarlathotep seemed puzzled by the same query, silent in his continuous slow approach.

"Based on the dreams, humans created a whole cultural cornucopia of literature and art," Malia continued. "But… they never yielded absolute control over their nightmares to you. Think of Derleth, and you will begin to understand."

Frowning in bafflement, Nyarlathotep cocked his head. Conflicting emotions warred on his animated face—his distinct desire for victory, his obvious need to defeat and humiliate her, *and* his clearly growing desperation. Shay witnessed the visible play of emotions, in awe of Malia's subtle influences on the mental state of those around her. "You speak nonsense."

"We are all creatures of madness, dear brother," Malia retorted with a wicked laugh. "Haven't you figured it out yet? Poor boy." Her sad pouty face was as false as the most outrageous lie. Nyarlathotep crouched slightly, as though about to pounce. "You created dreams; humans created flights of fancy based on them; and finally you created Innsmouth based on the subconscious images of humans and their gruesome, mad nightmares."

In shock, Shay drew in a sharp breath. The small fishing town of Innsmouth, MA, was nothing but a… a *dream…*? The very notion seemed to stem from mountains of madness.

"And here we are, traipsing inside a dream bubble warping time and space around us, like children playing with and reshaping putty," Malia said, her hands spreading to her sides as Nyarlathotep's had a moment ago. But where his had been a show of ego, her gesture spoke of a cool level-headedness apparently beyond him. "The shape of humans' dreams was an obstacle you could not pass. You had no choice but to follow the form of their imaginings to the letter."

A flicker of fear passed over Nyarlathotep's face like a cloud.

Malia's exultant smile shone as bright as the sun. "You created Innsmouth as a precise replica of the stories. Too exact, in fact. But I sympathize with your plight, brother. You had limitations placed upon you. You had no choice in the matter. Now you're reaping the rewards of the seeds you planted so long ago."

Without conscious awareness of the act, Shay spoke before his reason caught on to the idea that this probably wasn't the best time to be vocal. "This is all a dream?"

Malia didn't so much as glance in Shay's direction. Yet she answered. "Yes and no. In the stories, humans were forced to intermarry with and produce offspring for these immortal undersea creatures. Thus was created the so-called Innsmouth look: half-man, half-fish." Shay grimaced, disgust vibrating through his body and mind. "As children, these hybrids retained their humanity. Hybrids like me. But as they grew older, they transformed into deep-sea creatures. Hence the secrecy that permeated this society, hinted at in literature, as the elderly were hidden away, unseen, as the monsters they truly were."

"Monsters...." Nyarlathotep's growly whisper almost went unnoticed.

Apparently nothing escaped Malia's attention. "But you couldn't recreate humanity, brother, not in any sense of the word. That's why even the children Dev and I saw in town, such as Misery, didn't look human. Created from nightmarish images and vivid but wholly inaccurate phantasms, their humanity twisted and broken, they have virtually nothing in common with their counterparts. There's barely anything to provide even a semblance of normalcy. You couldn't control your own creations, which is why these hybrids needed the Echeneci. You may have made manifest all of humans' instinctual, basic fears, but you do not rule them."

"We'll improve in the future, then," Nyarlathotep said, his tone assured of his eventual triumph. "Thank you, sister, for your valuable advice. We will not forget." His comment was clearly aimed at the humans present, Shay concluded, and tried not to glare, not against an ancient, malevolent, alien deep-sea being.

"Oh, brother, but you haven't yet heard the best part," Malia drawled, her voice smooth as velvet, beguiling Nyarlathotep's attention once more. "Innsmouth may be a mere fabrication, an illusion at best and a nightmare at worst, but it is now real, caught in the here and now, subject to the laws of physics and nature. But behind the scenes… it is *we* who manipulate this dark reality. Our kind dominate this composition with our powers." Her cold chuckle resonated starkly in the tense ambience. "Oh, do excuse me. I meant, *my* powers."

Nyarlathotep laughed, seemingly at ease, as though there existed no threat from those opposing him. Shay would not have been so cavalier, not where Malia was concerned.

"I was right about you having recalled your powers," Nyarlathotep said. It appeared he was confident the revelation posed no danger to him. Shay puzzled as to why Nyarlathotep would assume so, given all the evidence to the contrary. Nyarlathotep's next words confirmed this. "Take care, sister. Omnipotence is exceedingly enticing, sweetly seductive—and ultimately quite corrupting. In no time at all you will grow to see our point of view—and only ours." His chin lifted in an act of arrogant presumption.

Shay almost felt for him. Almost. Empathy was another quirk of humanity this odious being neither recognized, felt, nor understood. He wasn't worth Shay's sympathy.

"This replica of your insidious influences and human imagination," Malia said, "has its drawbacks. We could go on at length about that. But I'll just focus on one." When she raised her chin, it was a bold act of confidence and defiance. Shay was certain they'd all be killed in seconds. "Unlike in Lovecraft's story, there was no government siege or subsequent raid back in 1928. Why? Because there was no real town back then. But now… Innsmouth does exist, as real as you or I." Her grin turned feral, a predator within sight of its prey. Shay sensed a tipping point was imminent, and so was their fate. "Innsmouth exists, thanks to you, Nyarlathotep. As do the unused explosive charges at Devil's Reef."

Nyarlathotep's eyes widened and his gaze snapped from Malia to the sea, toward the western horizon where the rocks of a faraway reef could be seen, gently cropping upward from the ocean floor. "*No…!*"

Malia growled like an animal and crouched slightly, both of her weapons aimed at his chest. "With those explosives, and with the flames of the cosmos that run through my hybrid being, I will rain fire and brimstone upon you and these wretched ruins and subcreatures, burying them for all time. History will forget you. You gave me the power to manipulate this fiction you created when you restored my alien memory, so do not be surprised by my actions now… dear brother."

WITHOUT WAITING for Nyarlathotep to refocus on her, Malia brought up her stunshine rifle, along with another gun Shay had never seen before, and fired. Shay was familiar with the blast, the high-intensity light that blinded, disoriented, and even overloaded the nervous system.

The second the blast hit Nyarlathotep, he cried out in pain and fell to his knees on the shore, holding on to his head. His eyes were open—and burning. White flames shot out of his seared eye sockets, scorching his face and licking his skin. His shadowy braids returned to their normal state, but Shay wasn't foolish enough to believe he had been defeated.

Then Malia fired the other, hitherto unknown, weapon.

A bolt of lightning shot out of it and then splintered into a mesh of electrical surges, hitting Nyarlathotep dead-on. He flew through the air as though he'd been slammed by a giant's backhand. The flashing and rattling web of lightning struck Nyarlathotep all over and cocooned him, the hits like electric blue-pronged spikes and needles piercing his body at all angles. He screamed in pain and fury, trying to fight it, but seemed unable to resist.

"What the hell was that?" Shay asked, dumbfounded, staring at Nyarlathotep as he twisted in torment.

Malia grinned savagely. "My own design. I call it a voltaic gun." She brought it close to her face, admiration in her voice and gaze as both her eyes and her fingers caressed the shape lovingly. "Twelve electrical bolt cartridges." Her ruthless gaze landed on Nyarlathotep, who gasped and tried to stand though still writhing in agony. "I didn't get a chance to test it onboard yet. But I suppose we have now had a successful field test."

Using both weapons this time, she fired again at Nyarlathotep.

The act coincided with another huge explosion that caused the ground to tremble and shake. Out at sea, to the east, pieces of blown-up rock flew high into the night air, lit by a series of massive firestorms raging and sweeping across the reef. The black sky turned orange as the flames kissed it, reaching for the heavens. Darkness was but a dim memory as night turned into day.

Immediately after, an enormous bubble rose from the ocean beyond until it burst into showers of water and ash, carrying with it new explosions and wildfires, making the water hiss and churn as it rained down in clouds of steam. Whatever had been beneath the surface, Shay surmised, it was no more.

Scorched and smoking, his foul stench piercing the air, Nyarlathotep tried to crawl forward, his target Malia. Where his eyes had been, now two black, immolated holes stared. But his unending rage remained, clinging to him in a perversion of life.

Malia approached slowly, her step light and even playful, without a care in the world. Her joyous voice bubbled with glee as she addressed the incinerated man on the shore. His hair was burnt to cinders, mere singed nubs on his head. His clothes smoked and his skin blackened, with an occasional trail of blood soaking his clothes, his skin, and finally the ground.

"Remember me mentioning Derleth to you, brother?" Malia asked. "You should have left him out of the creation business. To balance the dark forces of the Deep Ones he wrote the Old Gods into existence. Or as I like to call them, the Shunned. See what they have bestowed upon me." She remained out of touching range but still hunkered close, her gaze as unwavering and cool as her voice. "Oh, brother, you gave life to the darkest dreams of mankind—but also their greatest hopes. Silly, silly." She wagged her finger at him, like a parent chiding a child.

Nyarlathotep wheezed and coughed, desperately clinging to life, clawing the dirt under him to pull himself forward, his fingernails half-torn and bloody. "You…. Man-fool…. The Old Gods…. Your powers…. You degrade yourself…."

Malia chuckled, shaking her head. "No. You did that, all by your lonesome. After you restored my memory, I knew all that I needed to know in order to vanquish you. You bestowed upon me the ability to manipulate this fantasy. You allowed me to stretch forth with my mind and set off the charges you didn't even remember were there."

She chuckled when Nyarlathotep's seared fingers gripped her ankle, the touch futile and empty of strength as they slid along the leather quite ineffectually. With ease she straightened up, kicked his grasping hand aside, and squatted down once more.

Her smile was wicked as Nyarlathotep stared at her fruitlessly with his blinded eyes. "Oh, and, brother? Almost forgot. I added a few twists to the plot myself."

An extensive series of explosions wracked the small fishing town of Innsmouth—and the skyships above it, sending their sole, cowardly occupants, the traitorous elderly, to their fiery deaths. Fires burned the buildings and structures, an ocean of flames spreading everywhere in tidal waves of yellow, orange, and red. The skyship balloons hummed and rippled in the grip of the hot winds, their fabric growing black, first singed, finally burning.

When the first balloon blew up, fire rained over the town. Droplets of flame spattered around and hit the other skyships in close proximity. In a heartbeat they were all aflame. The first ship tilted and creaked loudly, barely heard over the roar and rumble of the conflagration advancing through the already-ruined town.

Then the skyship came down like a burning missile, crashing into what used to be the center of town. The remaining crafts soon followed, raining down on the town like gods falling from the sky. The ground shook under their feet, rumbling and roaring like a mighty beast waking to life. Like fiery wheels set in motion, the rounded skyship hulls spun on their axes as they rolled downhill, setting whatever was left of the town aflame and crushing everything in their path.

The smoke, soot, and ash summoned forth the rain from the gathering dark blue clouds, and it fell hard and sharp like pins and needles. The cold downpour pelted Innsmouth, but the gush was not enough to extinguish the fires. In an instant, Innsmouth was nothing more than an inescapable inferno. The screams of the remaining residents were barely audible over the din of destruction.

It was Dev who first saw the danger of the plan. Though they were lit up with flames and smoking, the remaining Innsmouthian people emerged from the blazing wreckage toward the shore, murder their sole goal.

Dev shoved Shay behind him and raised his rifle, shouting, "Time to go!"

His words might have been aimed at Malia, but she didn't move. She did see the last hurrah of approaching enemies and the final barrage of doom as the few skyships left rained ruin upon the imaginary town.

But Malia's main focus was on Nyarlathotep, who still hadn't yielded. Agonizingly slowly, he crept across the shore toward her. An indecipherable gurgle escaped his throat. Shay was sure it wasn't a plea for mercy.

Dev rushed to her side and gripped her arm, twisting her to face him. "Malia, we have to go. Now. Finish him so we can leave." He didn't wait for her response. He waved anxiously at Shay to follow as he headed past the ruined lighthouse to get to the ladder up to the airship. He let his stunshine rifle do the talking as one of the last surges of Innsmouthian menaces rounded the lighthouse and rushed at him and the few rangers still defending the rope ladder and their only access to the last remaining airship still in the air.

Shay hurried to Malia, who watched silently, blankly, as Nyarlathotep wormed his way now toward the bay waters instead of her. "Malia, please, come with us," Shay pleaded, his hand gentle on her shoulder. His gaze flicked over to the few Innsmouthians still left to do battle, though it was obvious they had lost. "Malia."

As Nyarlathotep's fingers finally immersed in the shallow waters of the bay, Malia shook her head, still watching only her enemy. "No, Shay. I'm not coming with you. You must go. Your people await. You must live to fight another day."

Nyarlathotep's head sunk under the waves. Shay had a feeling if he got all the way to his underwater lair, if such a thing even existed, he would survive, somehow, to become a plague on their existence once more.

Malia seemed to be thinking along the same lines. Calmly she raised both her weapons and shot Nyarlathotep in the back. He could no longer cry out, his voice too hoarse, his throat clogged by water and fire. With his hands, he attempted to shield his head, but his agony was plain to see.

Shay trembled in disgust. "Malia, we aren't like him. Don't torment him."

Blinking, she raised her hazel eyes at him. Slowly a flicker of a smile emerged from the depths of her darkness. "You truly are the best of men," Malia said, her tone sad but proud too. "You make me wish I was the best of women. Perhaps I have too much of them inside me after all." She pressed the voltaic gun into Shay's palm, wrapping his fingers around it. "This will aid you in the future, I'm sure. Have your mechanics reverse engineer it."

Nyarlathotep was unable to fully submerge himself. He twitched in place, huddled into a fetal position, which struck Shay as odd. Were immense, immortal deep-sea creatures even born in such a condition?

"He's been defeated," Shay said, a flood of sympathy overwhelming him despite the shivers of disgust and fear. "Slay him or not, but let us leave this horrible place. Let's go home." He heard the begging in his own voice but felt the situation warranted it.

Pressing the heel of her boot on Nyarlathotep's back to keep him from escaping, Malia regarded him with mournful regret. For a moment she seemed to be of two minds, but the moment passed quickly. "Shay, my dearest friend, I *am* home."

"But...." Shay shook his head in confusion and frustration. "That makes no sense. You said it yourself that you're more human than... whatever they are." He pointed at Nyarlathotep on the ground, writhing and groaning, his head half above the surface, half buried below it. He seemed to believe water would be his safe haven, which might have been true. But he couldn't advance, not with Malia's boot lodged on his back. "You've destroyed this town, dream or not," Shay insisted, despondent and dejected. "Where else would you go? You promised that you'd—"

Malia cupped his cheek tenderly, good-bye in her eyes. "Shay, love.... *Malia is already dead.*"

CHAPTER 13

IT TOOK every ounce of strength Dev had to grab Shay and drag him away from Malia and back toward the ship. He hollered orders to the rangers who were safe onboard to launch the ship on a course out of town. He couldn't climb the ladder with a resisting, struggling Shay in tow, but he clung to both the rung and to his beloved with all his might, of which there wasn't much left.

"No!" Shay shouted. "We have to go back for her. Malia!"

"We can't!" Dev yelled back, desperate to make Shay understand. "We'll all die." As the airship slowly rose higher, their feet left the ground as they dangled from the ladder. And just in the nick of time too.

The remaining scattered members of the Innsmouthian horde reached the spot they'd vacated. Though their expressions were blank of emotions, they wailed and shouted, their clothes in flames, their voices husky from smoke inhalation, their skin black and scorched. The squids on the backs of their skulls danced in the colors of the rainbow and faded slowly. The fish men snatched rocks from the beach and hurled them toward Dev and Shay, who could do nothing to defend themselves, holding tight to the ladder instead.

A sharp stone cut across Dev's forehead, stinging. Blood dripped into his eye, blinding him. He groaned in pain but was otherwise helpless against the final onslaught.

With his still-open good eye, he saw the black-haired little girl, Misery, join the scant few left alive. She had a blade, which she tossed through the air. With a low thump, it struck Dev in the thigh, sinking in almost to the hilt. Dev screamed then, his vision blurring, his head dizzy.

Dev felt his grip on Shay slipping.

Then Shay seemed to snap out of his funk and come to his senses. For he wrapped his arm around Dev's waist, holding on to him, keeping them both from falling. Shay placed his other hand on top of Dev's on the rung, their grip growing stronger together.

"Hold on, Dev," Shay murmured desperately. He was crying; Dev could hear it in his shaky voice. "I love you. I'm sorry. Please don't die. Hold on." Dev didn't get to answer as Shay shouted up to the airship and the rangers there, "Shoot them, damn you. Fire!"

Past them, stunshine blasts and collision grenades wreaked havoc among the surviving Innsmouthians. Their cries of pain soon subsided as they blew through the air, dropping like flies onto the pebbly beach, finally lying there unmoving and incinerating to cinders. Their colorful, sparkly squids darkened as well.

Beyond them, Innsmouth burned. Wreckages of skyships had torched the place good, leaving not a single building untouched by the blaze. No more sounds of living beings could be heard, no movement could be discerned. The town was dead, with only its funeral pyre left.

A grating sound of wooden wheels turning and crunching, and the creak of tightening ropes heralded the slow but steady ascent of the ladder. Dev could scarcely hold on. His body shook, and his muscles protested the prolonged exertion. He couldn't even keep his eyes open anymore. He was almost too tired to care if he fell to his death.

One last glance with his good eye gave him a vision of a rocky nighttime beach where a lone woman stood. Next to her, an immolated body lay still. *Nyarlathotep's dead? Finally a piece of good news.* Dev smirked to himself as he watched Malia wave and vanish into the depths of the bay. He wondered where she was headed now, if she would still live tomorrow.

What would become of her? Would she in time transform into a Deep One?

Would they one day have to do battle against *her*?

As Dev and Shay were pulled over the airship railing by the strength of several pairs of hands, Dev decided this was as good a moment as any to get some sleep. Blackness swept him up with swift wings into the land of dreams and nightmares.

SOFT WHISPERS and tiny sniffles brought Dev back from the dreamland of darkness and shadow. He felt heavy all over, too weary to lift a finger, let alone an eyelid. His head throbbed, his leg ached, and he wasn't sure if he was truly awake.

A gentle swipe of a cold, wet rag over his forehead told him his sensations were real.

A quiet voice murmured and beckoned, "Dev, please, please, be all right. I love you so much. I'll die without you. I'm sorry for everything. I should never have taken us to that wretched place. Too many died because of me. If you join their ranks, I'll…." His words failed and his voice faded into sobbing. The hand brushing against Dev's skin disappeared too.

Dev tried to get a grip on his fatigue and gravity to offer comfort to the only person he'd ever loved, his Shay. His own voice was nothing but a craggy, mumbling mess. "Shay, I love you too. 'S okay. No cry."

A sharp, startled gasp told Dev he'd been at least marginally successful in conveying his awakened state and his attempt at consolation to his beautiful young scholar.

"Dev?" Shay's small voice called out to Dev, shaking him out of his lassitude. "Dev, oh, I was so worried you'd never wake up." Kisses rained down on Dev's face, peppered all over his skin like the sweetest benediction. "I'm so sorry I nearly got us killed. Malia…." His affections ceased, but only for an instant. Then he kissed Dev on the mouth, insistent and invasive—in a good way. Shay seemed to pour all of his fears and losses into that one act of passion. If Dev could offer this support to the man he loved, that's what he'd do, and gladly.

After long moments of sweet, pleasurable kissing, Shay parted from Dev, sighing. "I love kissing you. We should have started doing that long ago."

"Agreed," Dev rumbled deep in his chest. Shay sighed again, contentedly this time. He spread out on the narrow cot in the captain's cabin of the airship, his warm, slender body next to Dev's. Shay rested his head on the nook of Dev's shoulder and neck, his arm slung haphazardly over Dev's broad, hairy chest.

"Where are we?" Dev asked.

Shay didn't raise his head. "Your cabin on the *Smoke Sparrow*. It's past noon. We'll be back in Canal City before sundown. Your thigh was injured quite badly by a blade, but it's now bandaged. You'll be okay. I promise."

Dev swallowed hard, replenished, thanks to Shay's kisses, but still restless and weary. The last couple of days had taken their toll on all of them. "How many…?" *How many survived?* But he couldn't speak the words out loud for fear he'd jinx potential good news.

Shay let out a small sob. "Forty-nine. Only young. None of the… elderly."

Dev closed his eyes tight. Forty-nine from seven skyships, each with a crew of twelve in addition to their elderly Sovereign Society passengers, likely three or four per ship. So forty-nine out of over a hundred. This expedition had taken them all to hell and back. Casualties were always a possibility but never an outcome one was adequately prepared for.

Shay's hot tears rained on Dev's skin. "I'm sorry, Dev."

"Not your fault." Dev hugged Shay closer. For a time they held on to one another like hanging on to a lifeline. Dev had read a phrase befitting their situation in a book once, or perhaps heard it from someone more knowledgeable. It said something along the lines that the darkest hour came just before a new dawn. He didn't think that was likely in the literal sense, but he did get the point of the proverb, the attempt to instill hope in one's most desperate moment. "I'm sorry too. I should have tried to save Malia."

This time Shay did raise his head, his glistening eyes filled to the brim with tears, his cheeks wet with their trails. "Even… even after what she said?"

"Yes." Dev smiled wanly at Shay, a sense of loss cutting deep in his heart. "I should have tried. For you."

Shay frowned, less vexed, more befuddled. "She was dead, Dev. Malia died the instant she touched that green monolith. She told us so herself, in her own words. I don't think she lied to us about that just to get left behind."

Dev looked up at the ceiling of his cabin. An old marine oil lamp swung gently from the support beam, casting shifting lights and shadows across the warm and welcoming cavernous space. Wood creaked and metal mewed ever so gently as the airship made its way back to the city where it was constructed. A familiar place did nothing to lift his spirits, even though it should have. They'd lost a lot, yes, but they had gained a lot too.

Why wasn't the balance of that awareness soothing his battered soul?

"Dev?" Shay whispered, caressing his bearded jaw tenderly. "I'm not mad at you for doing what you had to do. Before we even came along, Malia had already decided that, live or die, she would not be rescued with the rest of us. I can't hate you, Dev. Never that. You're my world, my heart, my sanity, my all."

Though Dev knew that in his heart, he feared Shay didn't really mean it. Shay's bond to Malia was as strong as ever, whether she lived somewhere in a dark and dangerous world out there or not. "When I brought you back to the ship, you—"

"I yelled and struggled like a madman. Yes, I remember." Shay sounded embarrassed and apologetic. Dev wasn't sure he liked it. But Dev was no longer sure who, if either of them, had been in the right at that moment. "It's stupid but… she did love me. And I loved her. And yet… we didn't love each other the right way. I mean, the way a true couple should, you know?" Shay was staring at Dev's chest, though probably not really seeing it, absentmindedly twirling Dev's coarse chest hairs with his fingers. The sensation felt amazing. "I thought…. I mean, I felt like I'd already broken her heart—though I actually hadn't—by falling in love with you. I wanted to at least save her life, to bring her home, and to be her friend and comrade." Shay appeared miserable and at a loss for words. "I just wanted to save her."

With an act of will rather than of strength, Dev touched Shay's jaw and lifted it so they could lock gazes. "Shay, you did save her. By showing her the best humanity had to offer. Love, kindness, friendship, honor, trust, and ethics. And… she saved herself too, I think. By choosing the less trodden path and the side of the underdog, and then taking action." Dev let out a soft laugh of awe and respect. "Malia's one heck of a woman. We're privileged to know her."

A sob emerged Shay's throat. His hand trembled as it covered his mouth, as if to stop any more from escaping. "Thanks, Dev. Thank you for speaking of her as though she's still alive."

Dev grinned back and winked. "How hard is that? That woman can survive anything thrown her way." He nodded to himself, trusting in the veracity of his own claim. "Yeah. She's still out there, fighting against darkness, depravity, and evil. I know it. I have faith in her."

Shay kissed him while smiling, and their teeth clanked a bit. "Me too. If anyone can make it, she can." His touch cooled Dev like fresh water and burned him like fire. Shay said, "You know, I read somewhere once that humans are social animals."

Dev frowned, baffled. "What does that mean?"

Shay kissed Dev softly. "I think it means we're stronger together, capable of greatness." He stilled briefly, appearing serious and pensive. "We've learned from this expedition that the veil of civility is thin indeed. Underneath the surface, we are beasts."

Dev snorted. "So? Malia's blood was both human and alien, and she saved us all from slavery, extinction, and death. Our primal heart isn't our worst quality, I assure you. Not a weakness but a strength. Malia proved that time and again."

"I guess you're right." Shay cocked his head, staring at Dev, looking scared. "What about… us?"

Dev frowned, confused. "What do you mean?"

Shay worried his bottom lip nervously. "Do you still wish to… with me, I mean?"

Dev laughed even though the rumbling hurt his lungs and ribs. "What kind of a foolish question is that, you silly sunbird? Of course I do. I love you."

Drawing a sharp breath, Shay practically bounced with glee, his widening grin spreading to his very being. "You mean it?"

"When I all but made love to you in the sewers, that wasn't proof enough for you?" Dev chided his beloved softly, pursing his lips and rolling his eyes.

Laughing with pure excitement, Shay nodded, a feverish dark glow rising in his eyes. "So, um...." Frowning in hesitation, Shay gave Dev a quick once-over. "Do you think you could, uh.... Are you well enough to.... What I mean to say is that if you feel up to it, would you maybe consider...." Shay seemed to be wholly incapable of finishing his thoughts.

Thankfully Shay's meaning came through crystal clear. Dev chuckled, his voice husky and equally randy. "Absolutely, love. Just... let's take it slow, shall we?"

Before Dev had even stopped speaking, Shay was nodding frantically, straddling Dev below the waist, and lowering his hot, nubile body on top of Dev, grinding his hips roughly. "Uh-huh. I promise to take it easy on you." Then he kissed Dev deeply and thoroughly.

In fact, kissing and other sensual and sexual acts remained their sole focus for hours on end as they entwined around each other naked, needy, and perfectly in love. And Shay did take it easy on Dev. For a few minutes in the beginning, anyway.

His mind blank, his eyes tired, and his patience waning, Dev stood nude at the window of his small dwelling, staring at Canal City stretching below. There was no glass in the window, but wooden shutters he'd bolted in himself. What winds the shutters didn't catch, the heavy drapes did. His home was warm even during the long, harsh winters, that season fast approaching.

Only a scarce few windows in the city shone with flickering gaslights. The sun had set a while ago, but the sky still glowed orange at the horizon. From his vantage point, however, Dev saw only the reflections off the tall buildings of metal and glass.

Of course, metal had rusted and glass shattered, but the city lived on. Rough seasons had led to the collapse of facades and poorly constructed buildings. Those tall spires that still stood were missing windows, doors, paint, vital little details here and there. Even concrete foundations showed signs of erosion and disrepair despite their residents painting the metal surfaces to ward off rust and wear.

The high-rise where he had his modest domicile was only occupied on the middle levels.

The first few floors, like the streets below, had flooded within hours of the Cataclysm. Drainage, cabling, and transportation tunnels beneath the city streets lost power to the pumps that kept them dry, and the barriers that kept the sea at bay broke beyond repair. The ocean had stormed in, its level rising and taking hold of most avenues and boulevards, the city now consumed with water. Where streets and roads weren't submerged canals, they were covered by grass, meadows, moss, flowers, bushes, trees, and foraging wild animals. Thick carpets of plants had conquered the city, covering stairs, doorways, cars, streetlights, buildings, rooftops, pretty much everything man-made.

The roofs of skyscrapers hadn't fared any better. As the copper lightning rods protecting the tall structures fell victim to extreme weather, lightning storms, winter freezes, and summer heat, they had eroded and rusted, useless to safeguard the roofs, which upon lightning strikes turned into towering infernos. The few that remained partially or wholly intact were structurally unsound and unsafe as living quarters, as the seasonal threats never really went away.

Much of Canal City was now inhabited, but at a cost. Storms and wildfires had raged in the city. Wooden structures had burned to charred cinders. Many lives had been lost in the first ten winters since the Cataclysm, even a few since then. Thus enriched by fire, plant life broke through cemented areas, finding a way through any type of barrier. Now vines and creepers of all sizes, in addition to moss and lichen, covered all structures still standing.

From his perch, Dev could see a few people still roaming along the wooden bridges that had been built to connect the high-rises above water level. That had been relatively easy since windows had crashed long ago, taking chunks of wall with them. With careful masonry work, they had become the new entryways to the bridges and thus the lifelines to connect each part of Canal City by a network of buildings cut through at midlevel. One could traverse the entire city via these buildings and bridges, not once getting his or her feet wet.

To Dev's left, Central Park had grown into a wilderness, spreading outward to the adjacent city blocks. Many predatory animals now dominated that untamed landscape. Birds and deer had come first, feral dog packs and growing wolf populations following. Over the past couple of winters, people had even seen cougars and bears emerging from the wild beyond the city via the highways, major thoroughfares, and big bridges.

In order to keep Canal City from succumbing to a dangerous wilderness or from becoming a mere skeletal remnant of a ghost town, the surviving populace worked hard to repair and fix what was broken and to repel and defeat the resurgence of wildlife. Not an easy task by any means. They were still very much in their infancy when it came to inhabiting a city this size. Dev was justifiably proud of their accomplishments as a newly disadvantaged species.

Dev kept his weight off his injured, bandaged leg, grateful that the blade wielded by a mad little girl had been a small one. He'd have to stay off his leg for a little while longer to heal. Considering he—and the *Smoke Sparrow*, currently undergoing retrofitting—weren't going anywhere anytime soon, he had plenty of time to recuperate.

But it had already been near a moon's cycle. He was itching to get back up in the air. He didn't like staying put, even if Canal City was home.

A pair of bed-warm arms slid around his waist and hugged him close. Shay pressed tight to his back, sighing in satisfaction. His sleep-roughened voice was sexy as sin. "Coming back to bed?"

The two of them now shared Dev's dwelling. They had only two rooms and a single bathroom, which they shared with two other people living on the same floor, but it was enough for their needs. They had a place to rest, a place to cook food, and a place to wash up, even if the water had to be brought up from the canal in buckets with the aid of a simple rope-and-pulley system and then boiled (distillation desalinated the seawater enough to drink and wash with). It wasn't an easy life, but it had its rewards, even in the routines required for basic survival.

"Yeah, in a while," Dev replied to reassure his lover and companion. He picked up one of Shay's hands, brought it up to his lips for a kiss, and then rested his own hands on top of Shay's.

Shay delivered an openmouthed kiss between Dev's shoulder blades, his full lips hot and wet, causing Dev to shiver as heat flashed through him. "I know you're feeling impatient and raw having to wait about like this. I know you want to get back in the air."

Dev smiled, though Shay couldn't see it. His beloved knew him well indeed. "Yeah, I guess I am. But as you're aware, I'm a patient man. Look how long I waited for you."

Dev didn't need eyes on the back of his head to tell Shay was smiling like a loon. He had a habit of doing that when Dev complimented him. It was endearing as hell. "Yes." His voice was small and shy. Yet he was nothing of the kind. Not really. His hips rocked back and forth ever so slightly. Shay was as naked as Dev, who could feel the nudge of Shay's erection against his cleft, the poke hardly unpleasant. "Are you worried about what the Council will decide concerning your suggestion?"

Dev cringed. "Yeah." He exhaled, feeling out of sorts. "We need to figure out the full extent of influence those undersea creatures have on our world. We must locate and destroy all the places mentioned in those books. If they exist." He could only hope.

Shay rounded Dev until they faced each other. Shay's arms never left Dev's waist. His eyes were solemn and absolutely stunning. "I will back you up all the way, you know that. If Malia didn't die as Innsmouth went down in flames, she's undoubtedly doing the same on her end."

There had been no word from Malia in a moon's cycle. Though Dev had his doubts about Malia's demise, he wasn't holding his breath waiting for news from her. She had chosen her path. Though their goals converged, their paths diverged. She had made her decision to steer clear of humans, for the time being anyway. On the one hand, Dev could understand her rationale; on the other he questioned it. Surely she would always be welcome among them.

"The Council has wise men and women, but they're understandably ambivalent about expending scarce resources on uncertain expeditions. I get that. Canal City and its people must come first." It wasn't that Dev didn't believe in his own words. But he did ponder the futility of arguing the importance of their case before the Council, who had not seen what Dev, Shay, and other rangers had. He glanced down at Shay. "Do you think other towns like Innsmouth could indeed exist out there in the wild?"

Shay shrugged, but his expression hardened. Hatred toward the alien fiends who had cost him his friend's life still burned, Dev knew. "I'm a scholar. And… I've seen things no sane person would believe. So yes, I believe anything is possible. And you're right. We need to be prepared for that contingency."

Dev grew weary of talking about dead friends, alien enemies, and burned towns. He sought solace, and had no uncertainty about where to find it. *Love.* He smiled as he brushed the tip of his nose against Shay's. "Come, love. Let's go to bed. Tomorrow morning will be a new dawn, with or without us worrying about every damn thing under the sun."

Red slashed across Shay's cheeks and neck as he blushed cutely. Dev didn't wait. He slanted his mouth and took Shay's in a ravaging kiss that made chills run up and down his spine and his toes curl. Shay moaned sweetly, going slack in his arms and opening up for Dev's desire.

Dev cupped Shay's round, plump buttocks and lifted him onto his lap, all without breaking their kiss. Shay wrapped his legs around Dev's hips, crossing his ankles behind him, and hung on with the agility of a monkey. Dev had come to know well this side of Shay's personality, the ravenous beast hungry for sex. As the old adage went, it was always the quiet ones that were the wildest within.

Still waters run deep, Dev thought in passing as he carried Shay to their shared bed, laid him down, and covered him with his body.

A mutual sigh echoed in the otherwise bare room. They'd have the chance later to decorate their dwelling like a proper home.

Last night they had spent their energies and lust in a frenzy of passion; now they had the time and energy to go slow, to take loving care of one another, to explore and be rewarded with new discoveries.

Dev let his hands roam and grope, his fingers caress and shift, and his mouth delve deep and claim as his own. Shay arched into him, small sighs and tiny whimpers escaping him. He wound his arms around Dev's broad back and wide shoulders, scraping his nails on the taut flesh with savage abandon, leaving sharp marks of ownership. Dev approved.

In a heartbeat, they were moving in unison, rocking as one, riding waves of pure pleasure, swaying in the wake that led to rapture. Dev couldn't part with Shay's sweet mouth, his delicious taste exploding on Dev's taste buds, his musky male scent overwhelming his senses, his heat scorching Dev's skin.

Wanting and having combined; Dev knew he'd never be able to get enough of Shay, never enough to last a single lifetime. Their shared path would endure forever.

As their mutual gratification crested, they surfed on the tidal wave of delight to a pure paradise belonging only to those who allowed love to carry them there. Shay's apple-scented breath fanned hotly over Dev's sweaty skin, giving him goose bumps. Fruit was scarce, so Shay spoiled himself with a piece after each expedition, whether they recovered survivors or resources, or not. Coming back alive was a win in itself.

As they rested together, side by side, they slowly touched one another, not with sex as their goal, but simply to feel the other there, close enough to hear each other's heartbeats. Dev drew lazy circles on Shay's arm and hipbone, tracing the invisible lines where he'd kissed earlier.

Shay giggled and squirmed. "Tickles."

Dev looked at him, his smile as bright and true as the sun. With a single carefree word he'd entered Dev's heart, as though he hadn't already dwelled there and owned Dev to every degree. He couldn't stop staring, in awe of the beauty and perfection love freely gave to its followers. Since love could produce visions like this, Dev was a willing worshiper at the altar of Shay's sunshine.

Like levies breaking, words they had been afraid to share with each other before now spilled willingly, tumbling out of their mouths with affection and sincerity. In reverent and hushed tones, they whispered vows of love until they finally fell asleep in each other's embrace.

EPILOGUE

"As you're undoubtedly aware," Rook said, "the Council has gone through lengthy deliberations concerning this situation." Her gaze swept over her audience. "The losing of our memories in the Cataclysm is an event that can't be undone without these deep-ocean creatures. We have found their price too high to pay, which I'm sure you have already figured out on your own." Her dry grin was reflected on Dev's face.

Rook straightened up, her chin lifting. "We have also come to the conclusion that your suggestion shows the greatest merit. So we have decided against full disclosure to the populace about the Innsmouth case for the sake of the elderly left in the city who had nothing to do with the Sovereign Society and their dastardly designs. They're innocent in all this. Therefore it's our duty as leaders to protect them from harm."

Dev was exceedingly glad to hear the Council's resolution and wholeheartedly agreed with them. He couldn't and didn't try to stop the wide grin that threatened to split his face in two.

"However… we have further urgent news for you." Rook's voice never showed panic or distress. But a hint of tension had crept into the councilwoman's typically level tone.

The Council Hall was situated in what had once been the periodicals room in the New York Public Library, now renamed Canal City Library. The beautiful brown-toned room had huge arched windows, painted murals on the walls depicting notable publishers from centuries ago, and ornate wooden carvings abounding on the walls and ceiling.

A gaslight chandelier offered soft illumination over the desks and chairs, which were arranged in a circular pattern, allowing all eyes of the attendees to focus on the person speaking in the center.

At the moment, that person was Rook, a councilwoman who had been seven winters old at the time the Cataclysm struck. A strong-willed brunette, she was the heart of the Council in the eyes of many, though the Council was composed of equal members.

Of the twenty-five seats in the room, only five had occupants. Two of those were Dev and Shay; the other three—Marlin, Condor, and Panda—were councilmen and -women. These three, along with Rook, were in charge of the expeditionary projects, deciding where to travel, with how many, in what time allotted, and with what objectives.

Dev had dealt with them all extensively for many a winter as an airship captain. He considered them dispassionate, smart, focused, and dedicated. With their wise counsel and strong leadership, Canal City had grown into a safe haven for all survivors and prospered as a new beginning for human civilization. They weren't defeated yet.

Nonetheless, he noted the absence of many Council members, with over a dozen seats now permanently vacated of their former owners, who had been Sovereign Society supporters killed in Innsmouth. All those left had been children under ten when the Cataclysm happened, or hadn't even been born yet.

An inward sneer awoke his cynical self to grouse, not that it did any good, to ponder and mull in perfect hindsight, unable to change a thing without the aid of another fictional invention—a time machine.

"A lone scout returned this morning from the north. Prior to his homecoming, he had already warned us by sending a message via a clockwork carrier pigeon," Rook said, her voice composed, revealing nothing. Yet the lines of her mouth seemed starker than usual. "As you might be aware by now, we sent him out there to determine *and* to ensure that Innsmouth and its hybrid inhabitants were indeed decimated and wiped off the face of the earth."

Dev shifted anxiously forward on his seat, leaning his elbows over the wooden desk. "And?" He rarely stood on ceremony. But that didn't mean he didn't respect these people.

Rook nodded firmly. "The threat is contained. Innsmouth is gone." Dev closed his eyes in relief and released a breath he hadn't noticed he'd been holding. Next to him, Shay seemed to have a similar reaction. "However…," Rook continued. That certainly didn't sound promising, Dev mulled glumly, waiting with bated breath. "As the scout journeyed back, he came across lights at a location that matches one mentioned in the books and maps Shay provided us with. The ones that depict fictional cities and towns written about by Lovecraft, Derleth, or others."

"Which one?" Shay asked, his posture stiff and resolute. Dev was both proud of and worried about him. But he said nothing.

Rook's eyes flashed. "Arkham."

Dev didn't wait for the command. He stood up, grateful when his leg didn't protest the sudden movement. On instinct he checked that his knife and gun belt were in place and squared his shoulders. "When do we leave?"

By his side, Shay rose from his seat as well, his back straight and his eyes alight with determination. Dev could have kissed him. Once they got home, but before they left for the new trip, he'd do just that—and carry out a few other ideas he'd been toying with in his leisurely time off.

Rook's dour, lopsided grin spoke volumes. She was proud of them and their initiative. "Tomorrow. At first light. Your airship, *Smoke Sparrow*, is in the final stages of retrofit, with new stunshine and voltaic cannons installed. Additional armaments will be provided, and an expert team of qualified rangers will accompany you on your mission. And gentlemen?" She regarded Dev and Shay sharply but fondly too. "This time, I expect *all* of you to return safe and sound."

Both Dev and Shay nodded their understanding and compliance. As though their reply would have been any different.

Rook's pleased gaze upon them radiated esteem and respect. "We have built a brand-new civilization here in Canal City. We have a justifiable right to be proud of our accomplishments. Wars have ended, battles ceased, strife and hate become extinct. We represent a true global community. It is my most ardent wish that we will continue to live, endure, and evolve to better ourselves and create a lasting foundation for future generations." Her inspirational speech warmed

Dev's heart because she truly believed in her rhetoric. "With that in mind," she continued softly, "I wish you Godspeed."

Though the meaning of that last phrase had been lost in the turmoil of the Cataclysm, Dev nonetheless appreciated Rook's sentiment.

As they walked down the white stairs of the library building, its impressive facade of tall columns and stairs flanked by two lion statues at their backs, Dev grinned at Shay. "Ready?" he asked, enthusiastic about flying again, wind beneath them, only sky as their limit. Defeating a horde of alien enemies in the process was a pleasant bonus.

Shay grinned back mischievously, as if sensing Dev's excited mood, and seemed just as full of zeal and drive. With a salacious wink and a theatrical cocking of his stunshine gun before stuffing it back in his hip holster, he said, "I was born ready."

Dev's joyous laugh resonated around them as they bounded down the stairs to embark on their next adventure—into Arkham, Massachusetts.

Susan Laine, an award-winning, multi-published author of LGBTQ erotic romance and a Finnish native, was raised by the best mother in the world, who told her daughter time and again that she could be whatever she wanted to be. The spark for serious writing and publishing kindled when Susan discovered the gay erotic romance genre. Her book, *Monsters Under the Bed*, won the 2014 Rainbow Award for Best Gay Paranormal Romance.

Anthropology is Susan's formal education, and she could have been happy as an eternal student, but she's written stories since she was a kid, and her long-term goal is to become a full-time writer. Susan enjoys hanging out with her sister, two nieces, and friends in movie theaters, libraries, bookstores, and parks. Her favorite pastimes include pop music, action flicks, eating chocolate, and doing the dishes, while a few of her dislikes are sweating, hot and too-bright summer days, tobacco smoke, and purposeful prejudice.

Website: www.susan-laine-author.fi

E-mail: susan.laine@hotmail.com

Blog:

www.goodreads.com/author/show/5221828.Susan_Laine/blog

Facebook:www.facebook.com/Susan-Laine-128697277229180

Twitter: @Laine_Susan

BLUE
ON
BLACK
CAROLE
CUMMINGS

Kimolijah Adani—Class 2 gridTech, beloved brother, most promising student the Academy's ever had the privilege of calling their own, genius mechanical gridstream engineer, brilliantly pioneering inventor... and dead man. But that's what happens when a whiz kid messes with dynamic crystals and, apparently, comes to the attention of Baron Petra Stanslo. Killed for his revolutionary designs, Kimolijah Adani had been set to change the world with his impossible train that runs on nothing more than gridstream locked in a crystal. Technically it shouldn't even be possible, but there is no doubt it works.

Bas is convinced the notoriously covetous and corrupt Stanslo had something to do with Kimolijah Adani's tragic and suspicious end. A Directorate Tracker, Bas has finally managed to catch the scent of Kimolijah Adani's killer, and it leads right into Stanslo's little desert barony. For almost three years, Bas has tried to find a way into Stanslo's Bridge, and when he finally makes it, shock is too small a word for what—or, rather, whom—he finds there.

www.dsppublications.com

J. I. RADKE

ROOKS AND ROMANTICIDE

In an alternate world, Romeo and Juliet are gunslingers. Verona gives way to a steampunk Victorian London. The victims of turf wars are dumped in an alley they call Lovers' Lane, and the moment the son of his family's enemy touches his face, Cain's revenge is poisoned by love. Fate would have it no other way.

Levi Ruslaniv is the heir to the Ruslaniv family gang, but ridiculous ancient feuds do not interest him. Cain Dietrich's vengeful hatred for the Ruslaniv family is rooted deep, since he believes the Ruslanivs arranged for the murder of his parents. But his encounter with Levi pierces him deeper than hatred ever could.

With bullets and blazes of glory, schemes, spies, and pack mentalities, loyalty runs as deep in the veins as passion or revenge, and there is only one way to end the fighting. From the start it was inevitable—a bloodstained fate for children with bloodstained hands, and the streets of New London will never be the same.

Urban Fantasy from DSP Publications

DREAMLANDS
FELICITAS IVEY

Dreamlands: Book One

The Trust and its battle-hardened recruits are fighting a horrific war, a war between the humans of this world and the demons of the Dreamlands. In this shadowy battle, Keno Inuzaka is merely a pawn: first an innocent bystander imprisoned and abused by the Trust, then a captive of a demon oni when taken to the Dreamlands.

But oni Samojirou Aboshi treats the human with unexpected care and respect, and the demon only just earns Keno's trust when a team from the Trust arrives to exploit the Dreamlands' magic.

As the war spreads across both worlds, Keno is torn between them. If he survives, he faces a decision: go home and carve out a new life under the Trust's thumb... or stay in the Dreamlands and find freedom in love.

www.dsppublications.com

BLACK DOG BLUES

RHYS FORD

Ever since being part of the pot in a high-stakes poker game, elfin outcast Kai Gracen figures he used up his good karma when Dempsey, a human Stalker, won the hand and took him in. Following the violent merge of Earth and Underhill, the human and elfin races are left with a messy, monster-ridden world, and Stalkers are the only cavalry willing to ride to someone's rescue when something shadowy appears.

It's a hard life but one Kai likes—filled with bounty, a few friends, and most importantly, no other elfin around to remind him of his past. And killing monsters is easy. Especially since he's one himself.

But when a sidhe lord named Ryder arrives in San Diego, Kai is conscripted to do a job for Ryder's fledgling Dawn Court. It's supposed to be a simple run up the coast during dragon-mating season to retrieve a pregnant human woman seeking sanctuary. Easy, quick, and best of all, profitable. But Kai ends up in the middle of a deadly bloodline feud he has no hope of escaping.

No one ever got rich being a Stalker. But then few of them got old either and it doesn't look like Kai will be the exception.

www.dsppublications.com

T.A. VENEDICKTOV

CHRYSALIS CORPORATION

Chrysalis Corporation: Book One

Together, they can change the rules of the galaxy and the definition of humanity.

When Damion Hawk is offered an opportunity to escape the destitute life of a miner on Mars and become an elite Alpha Fighter pilot, he jumps at the chance. Within the Chrysalis Corporation, Damion must learn to work with his Core—a man with computerized implants, no human emotions—and no rights. But unlike other Fighters, Damion can't treat Core 47 as a tool. He sees 47 as more than a machine, and he'll take deadly risks to help 47 find the humanity inside him.

Fighters and Cores are designed to work together and enhance each other's strengths in defense of their employer. Damion and 47 will need each other's support as suspicions about the all-powerful Chrysalis Corporation arise. Someone wants Damion and 47 gone, and they need to find out who and why while hiding 47's growing emotions and the love forming between them. If they can succeed, they might save not only themselves, but all Cores enslaved by the Corporation.

www.dsppublications.com

CASTO
GODS OF WAR
XENIA MELZER

Gods of War: Book One

All is fair in love and war. Renaldo has lived happily by that proverb his entire life. But he has finally met his match, and he's about to discover how unfair love and war can be.

When demigod and warlord Lord Renaldo takes a beautiful stranger captive during an ambush, he is delighted to have found a distraction that will keep him entertained during the upcoming siege. Little does he know, Casto is keeping more than just one secret from him. Slowly, Renaldo gets sucked into a turbulent roller-coaster relationship with his mysterious prisoner, one that begins with hatred and soon spirals into a whirlwind of conflicting emotions. And when it seems that things can get no worse, an old enemy stirs right in the heart of his home.

Determined to keep Casto by his side, Renaldo has to find a balance between the capricious young man and his own destiny as a ruler and god to his people.

www.dsppublications.com